NEW PENGUIN SHAKESPEARE
GENERAL EDITOR: T. J. B. SPENCER
ASSOCIATE EDITOR: STANLEY WELLS

1.50

WILLIAM SHAKESPEARE

*

MEASURE
FOR MEASURE

EDITED BY
J. M. NOSWORTHY

PENGUIN BOOKS

ISBN: 9780143131731

Penguin Books Ltd, Harmondsworth, Middlesex, England
Viking Penguin Inc., 40 West 23rd Street, New York, New York 10010, U.S.A.
Penguin Books Australia Ltd, Ringwood, Victoria, Australia
Penguin Books Canada Ltd, 2801 John Street, Markham, Ontario, Canada L3R 1B4
Penguin Books (N.Z.) Ltd, 182–190 Wairau Road, Auckland 10, New Zealand

This edition first published in Penguin Books 1969
Reprinted 1972, 1974, 1976, 1978, 1979, 1980, 1982, 1983,
1984, 1985, 1986, 1987

Made and printed in Great Britain by
Richard Clay Ltd, Bungay, Suffolk
Set in Monotype Ehrhardt

CONTENTS

INTRODUCTION

No play of Shakespeare's more amply vindicates the claim that 'he was not of an age but for all time' than does *Measure for Measure*, even though in some respects it is a dated play. Its plot and much of its religious, moral, and political thinking belong to a Jacobean context into which we may find it difficult to project ourselves and with which we are not always wholly in sympathy. But in its subtle probing into human behaviour and its understanding of the complex circumstances that regulate man's actions and attitudes, it proclaims itself a surprisingly modern work.

The growth of our understanding of human life has been a gradual process and the German philosopher Wilhelm Dilthey has claimed that it is something for which we stand indebted to the poets. Dilthey, writing in 1895, distinguished three stages in the growth of such knowledge:

'The first stage is represented by Homer, who already makes it his business to understand life in terms of itself rather than in theological terms. He sees how men's actions and destinies are determined in the last resort not by the gods, but by their own passions and characters; and he portrays various outstanding *types*. Homer's characters, however, are all of one piece, and do not grow. The next stage comes with Shakespeare, who understands the impulse of the human mind towards the full *development* of its powers, and sees how this can sometimes lead to inner conflict and disruption. His types are active and dynamic. The third stage is represented by Schiller, who grasps the influence upon this inner development of the *outer circumstances* in which the hero stands, and sees him as fundamentally a historical phenomenon. His *Wallenstein* interprets its hero with an insight so profound that history can only accept and confirm it. The same outlook is now universally prevalent in poetry and the novel.'

(H. A. Hodges, *The Philosophy of Wilhelm Dilthey*, 1952, pages 234–5)

Meanwhile, a younger contemporary of Dilthey, the Swedish dramatist August Strindberg, was already establishing a further stage in the understanding and presentation of human behaviour. In the preface to *Miss Julie* (1888) he repudiates the homogeneity that informs the dramatic characters of his predecessors on the ground that vice has a reverse side closely resembling virtue, so that an author must refrain from passing summary judgement upon his creatures. In real life, he argues, events spring from a whole series of more or less deep-rooted motives from which the spectator isolates either the one that he is best able to understand or the one most flattering to his own reasoning powers. Concomitant with this renunciation of the single motive and the constant viewpoint is the claim that in dramatic dialogue, again as in real life, the cogs of one mind should engage those of another, so that no topic is finally exhausted.

If *Measure for Measure* appears thoroughly modern in outlook, this is because it fully exploits all these insights into human behaviour, looking before and after. Angelo, searching his own heart, recognizes that the threat to his self-supposed moral security resides not in Fortune and the stars but in his own character. He is made subject to growth and change, as also are Duke Vincentio and Isabella, and, to a lesser extent, Claudio and Mariana. But it is also made apparent that these mutations of character, with their tensions, disruptions, and ultimate resolution, are closely linked with historical circumstance – that is, with the desperate social and moral conditions of Vienna, which constitute something more than a mere background to the play. The characters who thus act and are acted upon exhibit the kind of moral ambiguity to which we are accustomed in so much contemporary writing. Vincentio is a good man who is, nevertheless, not seen to be essentially good in quite the same way as Brutus or even Hamlet. Isabella's virtue, though commensurate with that of Cordelia, is nevertheless more flawed and vulnerable. Angelo, though accorded the same potential for evil as Iago, is granted a relish of salvation that is sometimes strangely moving. With him our impulse is to understand and, in some measure, to sympathize.

Throughout the play we remain acutely conscious of the way in which the attitudes of any one of the characters affect those of others, and yet, though the action itself is neatly resolved, the morality relating to those attitudes remains a topic that is not finally exhausted. Shakespeare poses problems and supplies answers. But he does not presume to offer a definitive solution.

If *Measure for Measure* sorts better with the innovations of Schiller and the allegedly revolutionary aims of Strindberg than with the tastes of Dr Johnson and Coleridge, the explanation may well be that it is one of those masterpieces so much in advance of their time that the critical principles by which they can be judged have only recently emerged, and that, perhaps, not in their entirety. Both the stage-history of the play and its treatment at the hands of critics suggest that for three centuries its popularity was extraordinarily spasmodic, but the salient point for the present-day reader is that it is now more highly regarded than ever before. Modern criticism has brought to light significances which the play had never been thought to possess, and various quite recent revivals, some of them indebted to that criticism, have revealed that, as a stage piece, *Measure for Measure* is rich, coherent, and intensely vital. Future critics will perhaps recognize, more clearly than we, that this play has particular relevance to the shifting values and circumstances of the twentieth century. It is possible too that, when confronted with the more extreme of contemporary claims, they will accuse us of having overvalued it. The reader may do well, therefore, to guard against an excess of either adulation or denigration, and to accept *Measure for Measure* as the great masterpiece which it undoubtedly is without invoking ultimately damaging comparisons with such plays as *Hamlet*, *Othello*, *King Lear*, *Coriolanus*, or *The Winter's Tale*.

Judgement is difficult because *Measure for Measure* is probably the most complex and even the most contradictory of Shakespeare's works. All the other major plays, with the possible exception of *Troilus and Cressida*, submit to an acceptable general audit, but with *Measure for Measure* there exists no single agreed formulation of what the play actually does or how well it does it. Like a kaleidoscope it presents a different pattern every time we look into it. One reading may leave the impression of an uncompromising earnestness of purpose, while another may suggest the liberation of something essentially comic. We may respond on one occasion to its powerful religious significances, and on another to its deep concern with the principles of government. Its bawdry may, at times, seem an affront, yet appear, at other times, inoffensive. Isabella may impress as a cold symbol of chastity only to emerge, at the next scrutiny, as an all too worldly specimen of womanhood, and we are liable to interpret Angelo alternately as a pure Machiavellian stage villain and as a man who, being wrought, is perplexed in the extreme. The ambiguities are almost countless, and increased familiarity only serves to emphasize that one conception is inseparable from another.

*

The complexity of *Measure for Measure* is attributable in part to the period of its composition. The official Revels accounts show that *Mesur for Mesur* by 'Shaxberd' was presented at Court on 26 December 1604, but no other records relating to the play have survived. A year earlier, Shakespeare's company, which had hitherto acted under the patronage of the Lord Chamberlain, came under that of King James himself, and the newly styled King's Players, though still pursuing their normal activities at the Globe Theatre, found themselves called upon to make fairly frequent appearances at Court. James's own interest in drama seems to have been at best spasmodic, but his consort, Anne of Denmark, was enthusiastic and is known to have had a liking for new plays. It is reasonable, therefore, to infer that *Measure for Measure* was written some time during the summer of 1604 and that it had been carefully rehearsed and successfully presented at the Globe before being used to grace the royal Christmas festivities. This performance version may have differed, in greater or lesser degree, from the solitary early text preserved in the Shakespeare Folio of 1623 (see An Account of the Text, p. 185). There are minor imperfections and inconsistencies, but the received version is, on the whole, dextrous and coherent, and there is no warrant for supposing that there have been serious losses.

It was once held that during Elizabeth's reign Shakespeare's concern was with light-hearted comedies that reflected his own carefree attitudes, but that the arrival of James either coincided with or promoted a crisis of pessimism which directed him towards tragedy. Such a view could admittedly explain why the Jacobean *Measure for Measure* is so much more sombre and contemplative than the Elizabethan *Twelfth Night*, but it has few adherents nowadays. James was a wretched monarch, but defects that are obvious to us are unlikely to have been apparent to most of his contemporaries, and there are no grounds for supposing that his accession impaired either Shakespeare's fortunes or his general outlook. It is more reasonable to suppose that, responding instinctively to public taste, he normally worked in a particular genre over a certain period. The years 1590–1600 were pre-eminently those of the chronicle histories and of romantic comedies whose primary object was to extract delight and laughter from the adventures and misadventures, the pangs and foibles, of young lovers; 1604–8 were the years of tragedy, and thereafter his preoccupation was with the so-called dramatic romances in which he turned once more to young people in love, setting them in a fairy-tale atmosphere, subjecting them to a more searching probation and presenting them as idealized characters who excite sympathy but seldom provoke laughter.

It is in the years 1600–1604 that we find it difficult to detect a pattern. The energies liberated and most effectively exploited in *Julius Caesar* in 1599 led directly, a year or so later, into the massively reflective tragedy of *Hamlet*. Immediately afterwards, traditionally at Queen Elizabeth's command, Shakespeare went to the opposite extreme in *The Merry Wives of Windsor*, and then took his leave of romantic comedy in *Twelfth Night*. There followed *Troilus and Cressida*, a play which, for more than three hundred and fifty years, has defied all attempts at classification, *All's Well that Ends Well*, and *Measure for Measure*. These, it seems, were Shakespeare's least productive but most varied years.

What is perhaps most striking in this period of extraordinary diversity is the way in which one genre affects another. It is clear that, during these years, Shakespeare often paused to consider curiously and, leaving aside unverifiable conjectures about personal or national security, we may infer that, in the period that culminated in the writing of *Measure for Measure*, he assumed a strenuous and thoughtful attitude to life consonant with the spirit of the time. The publication in 1597 of Bacon's *Essays*, the product of a philosophic and scientific mind, was symptomatic of a new preoccupation with morality, which, according to John Hoskyns, now became the favourite Court topic. The emergent spirit of inquiry now became apparent in the gravity of George Chapman and the abrasive social criticism of Ben Jonson. Shakespeare, too, assumed new attitudes, and the ethical issues freely exploited in *Hamlet* are maintained in the succeeding plays and brought into prominence in *Measure for Measure* – which, of all the comedies, emerges as the one most widely concerned with the principles of good and evil. It might possibly be designated moral comedy, or even moral romance (in so far as it anticipates the values that inform Shakespeare's final plays), but no single term seems adequately to cover all that it achieves.

*

Measure for Measure is one of the handful of Shakespeare's works that are known to have been based on pre-existing plays. Its main source was George Whetstone's

History of Promos and Cassandra, 'divided into two Comical Discourses', written in 1578. The play was printed in the same year but failed to achieve performance, though its author, in his preface, makes it clear that it was intended for the stage Subsequently he refashioned his material in the form of a *novella*, which was printed in his *Heptameron of Civil Discourses* in 1582. The story had long been extant and had been written in very choice Italian by Giraldi Cinthio in his collection of prose romances, *Gli Hecatommithi* (1565), and also in his tragi-comedy, *Epitia*, published in 1583 ten years after his death. The relationship between the Cinthio and Whetstone versions is obscure and need not concern us here. The salient point is that Shakespeare was familiar with several forms of the story, so that it was Whetstone's prose narrative, for instance, which supplied the names of Isabella and Crassus, while other incidental debts have been traced to Cinthio. These do little or nothing to affect the claim that *Promos and Cassandra* should be regarded as the primary narrative source, save for the bedtrick involving the substitution of Mariana for Isabella, which serves to complicate the received story and which Shakespeare, with ultimate obligations to Boccaccio's *Decameron*, had already used in a different way in his own *All's Well that Ends Well*.

Whetstone's play tells how, in the Hungarian city of Julio, the laws against fornication, which had long since been disregarded, are invoked with extreme severity against a certain Andrugio by the King's deputy, Promos. When Andrugio's beautiful and virtuous sister Cassandra intercedes Promos temporarily relents, but subsequently makes the reprieve conditional upon her surrendering her body to him. She refuses at first, but is afterwards persuaded by Andrugio's pleas and assents to Promos's terms provided that he will first pardon her brother and then marry her. Promos thereupon has intercourse with her, but repudiates his promises and orders a gaoler to present Cassandra with the severed head of Andrugio. The gaoler substitutes the mangled head of a newly executed felon, which Cassandra takes to be that of her brother. She straightway informs the King, who rules that Promos shall first marry Cassandra and then be beheaded. As soon as the marriage has been solemnized, however, she discovers that she genuinely loves him and pleads for his life to be spared. This the King refuses until Andrugio, who has been present in disguise, reveals himself; both he and Promos are then granted a free pardon.

Shakespeare handled his source with characteristic freedom. He converted the shadowy King of Hungary into Duke Vincentio and made him not only chief promoter of the action of the play but also its hero. By turning the heroine, Cassandra, into the novice, Isabella, he was able to develop her into a much more complex and fascinating character, and, by adding the new figure of Mariana and utilizing the bed-trick, he gave the villain of the piece an altogether different emphasis. These and other changes all make for intense complication, and there can be little doubt that Shakespeare deliberately built up the problems for the sheer joy of resolving them. For outright virtuosity the dénouement of this play is exceeded only by that of *Cymbeline*, and it may be observed, since it has already been suggested that *Measure for Measure* foreshadows the late romances, that there is a degree of kinship between the two plays. Although we may affirm that *Cymbeline* is a dramatic romance and *Measure for Measure* is not, the analogy goes some way towards eliminating the need to regard the latter play as tragi-comedy, 'dark' comedy, or problem drama, and admits the provisional judgement that Shakespeare's preoccupation was with the particular kind of comedy that he found exemplified, however crudely, in Whetstone's play.

Promos and Cassandra belongs to the teething-time of English drama, and judgement of it craves a fair measure of charity, for it is desperately long and its dialogue is uniformly dull. Yet Whetstone's failure lies in the execution rather than the conception. He presents his main plot coherently and efficiently, and introduces a number of minor characters who furnish a crudely realistic background of sexual and general moral corruption. Shakespeare, whose attitude to his source-material was invariably both generous and shrewd, let the main plot serve as a spur to his imagination, abandoning much of his source once he had got under way and freely developing the background in accordance with his own needs. *Measure for Measure*, therefore, makes deliberate use of its prototype's two main components, and there is a marked similarity of basic structural pattern, though this is something which is perhaps obscured by the very manner in which the work of an honest plodder is transmuted. The nature of this transmutation can be sufficiently illustrated by citing Whetstone's rendering of Promos's temptation – a passage that well typifies the best that *Promos and Cassandra* has to offer:

> *Do what I can, no reason cools desire.*
> *The more I strive my fond effects to tame,*
> *The hotter (oh) I feel a burning fire*
> *Within my breast, vain thoughts to forge and frame.*
> *O, straying effects of blind affected love,*
> *From wisdom's path which doth astray our wits,*
> *Which makes us haunt that which our harms doth move,*
> *A sickness like the fever hectic fits,*

Which shakes with cold, when we do burn like fire.
Even so in love we freeze through chilling fear,
When as our hearts doth fry with hot desire.
What said I? Like to hectic fits? Nothing near.
In sourest love some sweet is ever sucked.
The lover findeth peace in wrangling strife,
So that if pain were from his pleasure plucked,
There were no heaven like to the lover's life.
But why stand I to plead their joy or woe,
And rest unsure of her I wish to have?
I know not if Cassandra love or no:
But yet admit she grant not what I crave,
If I be nice to her brother life to give,
Her brother's life too much will make her yield.
A promise, then, to let her brother live
Hath force enough to make her fly the field.
Thus, though suit fail, necessity shall win.
Of lordly rule the conquering power is such.
But, O sweet sight, see where she enters in:
But hope and dread at once my heart doth touch.

The naked frailties of this passage are mercilessly exposed when it is set beside Angelo's conflict of conscience at II.2.162–87:

What's this? What's this? Is this her fault or mine?
The tempter, or the tempted, who sins most?
Ha?
Not she, nor doth she tempt; but it is I
That, lying by the violet in the sun,
Do as the carrion does, not as the flower,
Corrupt with virtuous season. Can it be
That modesty may more betray our sense
Than woman's lightness? Having waste ground enough,
Shall we desire to raze the sanctuary

> *And pitch our evils there? O fie, fie, fie!*
> *What dost thou? Or what art thou, Angelo?*
> *Dost thou desire her foully for those things*
> *That make her good? O, let her brother live:*
> *Thieves for their robbery have authority*
> *When judges steal themselves. What, do I love her,*
> *That I desire to hear her speak again,*
> *And feast upon her eyes? What is't I dream on?*
> *O cunning enemy that, to catch a saint,*
> *With saints dost bait thy hook. Most dangerous*
> *Is that temptation that doth goad us on*
> *To sin in loving virtue. Never could the strumpet*
> *With all her double vigour, art and nature,*
> *Once stir my temper; but this virtuous maid*
> *Subdues me quite. Ever till now,*
> *When men were fond, I smiled and wondered how.*

Whetstone, as *Promos and Cassandra* and his other writings show, was greatly preoccupied with morality in the context of both human relationships and the workings of the body politic. The title-page of his play announces that:

> *In the first part is shown the unsufferable abuse of a lewd magistrate; the virtuous behaviours of a chaste lady; the uncontrolled lewdness of a favoured courtesan; and the undeserved estimation of a pernicious parasite.*
>
> *In the second part is discoursed the perfect magnanimity of a noble king in checking vice and favouring virtue.*
>
> *Wherein is shown the ruin and overthrow of dishonest practices, with the advancement of upright dealing.*

Further illustration, if more is needed, may be found in the preface, the argument, and even the text, which adds wise saws and moral instances in the form of marginal glosses.

This moral emphasis is, again, something which Shakespeare willingly adopted. In *Promos and Cassandra*, he clearly found a model which expounded those ideas which, at the time, he was himself intent on expounding. It is wrong therefore to suppose, as some critics have done, that the moral judgements which play such a conspicuous and important part in *Measure for Measure* are a purely Shakespearian innovation. It is simply that, in his source-play, he found a substantial body of moral philosophy which was wholly congenial to him, as it would have been to all those of his contemporaries who aspired to virtue, and that he accordingly decided to enrich and enlarge these received values.

However much Whetstone may have failed in execution, his aim was to convert the combination of plot, background, and moral and political philosophy into a particular kind of comedy, the essence of which he sets out in his dedicatory preface:

> *For to work a comedy kindly, grave old men should instruct, young men should show the imperfections of youth, strumpets should be lascivious, boys unhappy, and clowns should be disorderly; intermingling all these actions in such sort as the grave matter may instruct, and the pleasant, delight.*

Here Whetstone is substantially following the precepts for comedy current in his day. The several practices that he condemns were condemned two years later by Philip Sidney in *The Defence of Poesy*, where it is affirmed 'that the comedy is an imitation of the common errors of our life, which he representeth in the most ridiculous and scornful sort that may be; so as it is impossible that any beholder can be content to be such a one.' Such a view of the nature and function of comedy had already been expounded much earlier by Sir Thomas Elyot in *The Governor*:

> *First comedies, which they suppose to be a doctrinal of ribaldry, they be undoubtedly a picture, or, as it were, a mirror of man's life, wherein evil is not taught but discovered, to the intent that men beholding the promptness of youth unto vice, the snares of harlots and bawds laid for young minds, the deceit of servants, the chances of fortune contrary to men's expectation, they, being thereof warned, may prepare themself to resist or prevent occasion.*

This idea of comedy, still current at the time when *Promos and Cassandra* was written, is scarcely that which informs the work of Shakespeare's immediate predecessors, John Lyly, Robert Greene, and Henry Porter, nor does it hold for his own practice up to 1600, but these early formulas offer reasonably coherent statements of what *Measure for Measure* does and was evidently intended to do. It seems likely, therefore, that Shakespeare read or reread *Promos and Cassandra* around 1602; that he recognized in it a formula for comedy which, though different from that which he had hitherto followed, offered scope for the ideas that he was now concerned to express; that he thereupon followed Whetstone's design in *All's Well that Ends Well*, and went on to utilize both the old play and the old formula in *Measure for Measure*. This does not imply that he broke away completely from his earlier practice. In Shakespeare's dramatic career we can discern transitions but not revolutions, and with comic pattern, as with personal and political morality, he skilfully combined derived ideas with those which he had made very much his own.

*

The political thinking of *Measure for Measure* is based on the values accepted by most of Shakespeare's contemporaries and possibly by the dramatist himself. The play reflects the doctrine of degree or universal order as expounded by Ulysses in *Troilus and Cressida* and also the moral drawn from history by the chronicler, Edward Hall, that 'as by discord great things decay and fall to ruin, so the same by concord be revived and erected'. These views naturally receive their clearest absolute demonstration in the history plays which, in the 1590s, reveal the development of Shakespeare's political wisdom. The lessons then learned were not set aside when he turned to other genres, and his preoccupation with 'the unity and married calm of states' remains a ponderable motive in plays as diverse as *Hamlet*, *Antony and Cleopatra*, and *The Tempest*. It is not, by its very nature, a theme which can normally be given prominence in romantic comedy, yet *Measure for Measure* is there to testify that the science of government can be reconciled with the arts of love without detracting from a brilliant comic plot.

The state of Vienna is manifestly one in which great things have decayed and fallen to ruin, and it is from this that Shakespeare moves on to consider the problem of government and to offer revival and resolution in terms of justice and mercy. The operative antithesis is that between Vincentio, the excessively lenient governor, and Angelo, the excessively severe. Many commentators have been curiously blind to the fact that, in the purely political context, the Duke is no less reprehensible than Angelo. His controlling role in the play and his essentially virtuous nature do nothing to alter the fact that his long period of office has brought Vienna to the brink of moral anarchy, as he himself clearly recognizes:

We have strict statutes and most biting laws,
The needful bits and curbs to headstrong weeds,
Which for this fourteen years we have let slip;
                              ... so our decrees,
Dead to infliction, to themselves are dead,
And liberty plucks justice by the nose;
The baby beats the nurse, and quite athwart
Goes all decorum.

I.3.19–21, 27–31

Sith 'twas my fault to give the people scope,
'Twould be my tyranny to strike and gall them
For what I bid them do: for we bid this be done
When evil deeds have their permissive pass
And not the punishment.

I.3.35–9

My business in this state
Made me a looker-on here in Vienna,
Where I have seen corruption boil and bubble
Till it o'errun the stew. Laws for all faults,
But faults so countenanced that the strong statutes
Stand like the forfeits in a barber's shop,
As much in mock as mark.

V.1.314–20

The Duke's disregard for the rule of law, though basic to the plot, is nevertheless responsible for all the corruption – responsible, that is, for Lucio and his friends, for Pompey and Mistress Overdone, for Barnardine, and, conceivably, for the misdemeanour of Claudio and the helplessness of Escalus. It has countenanced Angelo's treatment of Mariana and has laid the way open for his monstrous intentions towards both Claudio and Isabella. The opening scene of the play emphasizes both Vincentio's impotence and his irresponsibility. That he delegates his powers to

22

Angelo, whose imperfections he apparently already knows, need cause us no concern, since this is necessary to the plot. Nor need his disguise trick, which has similar relevance. In any case this was a device which had long been recognized as permissible in a governor and there is nothing irresponsible or extravagantly romantic about a stratagem which, in the event, is indicative of a newly conceived awareness of duty, though the Duke's preliminary remarks (I.1.3–7):

> *Of government the properties to unfold*
> *Would seem in me t'affect speech and discourse,*
> *Since I am put to know that your own science*
> *Exceeds, in that, the lists of all advice*
> *My strength can give you . . .*

must give us pause. A governor, who, in an age when the divine right of kings was an article of faith, can freely proclaim that his ministers are better versed than he in the principles of government does not inspire confidence. One thing that *Measure for Measure* shows is how a thoroughly irresponsible ruler, partly through his own efforts and partly through the words and actions of others, belatedly learns his business and ends by conforming to the pattern of the ideal prince.

The strictly political implications of Angelo's part call for little comment. It may be, as Isabella charitably surmises (V.1.443–4), that

> *A due sincerity governèd his deeds*
> *Till he did look on me . . .*

but, as the play proceeds, we are shown how a Pharisaic insistence on the letter of the law is corrupted by power into a tyranny which eventually repudiates all laws and countenances murder. Politically, Angelo may be said to be a meaningful figure but not an extended one, and, as will be suggested later, it is from other aspects of his character that his interest derives.

*

With the themes of justice and mercy we reach the point at which the political merges into the personal, so that clear distinction is often impossible. What has been said in the preceding paragraphs sufficiently illustrates the concepts of justice attaching to the Duke and Angelo, the one a man in whom mercy has grown meaningless because it has degenerated into mere indulgence, and the other the frigid exponent of a justice which excludes mercy. Other characters are made to reflect some facet of justice. There is Escalus, no longer able to distinguish truth from falsehood, feebly advocating mercy and lapsing (II.1.37) into the vagueness of

heaven forgive him, and forgive us all

and (V.1.321) the parrot-cry of

Slander to th'state.

There is Elbow, who, with all the futility of a Dogberry, leans on a justice which sags under his weight. There is the gentle Provost, who advocates mercy but, because of his office, is powerless to fight for it. There is Lucio, whose distorted values yet admit a compassionate view of Claudio's alleged crime:

For that which, if myself might be his judge,
He should receive his punishment in thanks. I.4.27–8

Finally there is Isabella, who, when at the end of the play Vincentio is at last prepared to administer absolute justice, persuades him to mitigate its severity with a full measure of Christian charity.

The principles which Isabella invokes are those which Shakespeare had already invoked in earlier plays. Portia's famous speech in *The Merchant of Venice* offers a sufficiently clear statement of the belief that mercy must season justice, and this, in *Measure for Measure*, is both explicit (in Isabella's plea to Angelo, II.2.49–141) and implicit. Equally conspicuous is the companion principle that we should do as we would be done by – a sentiment voiced earlier by Lord Say in *2 Henry VI*, IV.7, by the Lord Chief Justice in *2 Henry IV*, V.2, and most notably in the scene which Shakespeare contributed to the play of *Sir Thomas More*. These principles, for which Isabella, despite her own lapses, is made chief spokesman throughout the play, are, as is well known, those expounded in the Sermon on the Mount. The account given in Saint Luke's Gospel 6.36–42 of Christ's development of the precept that we should love our enemies was the one that had widest currency in Shakespeare's day and was familiar to him in this form:

Be ye therefore merciful, as your Father also is merciful.

Judge not, and ye shall not be judged: condemn not, and ye shall not be condemned: forgive, and ye shall be forgiven.

Give, and it shall be given unto you: a good measure, pressed down and shaken together and running over, shall men give into your bosoms. For with the same measure that ye mete withal shall other men mete to you again.

And he put forth a similitude unto them: Can the blind lead the blind? Do they not both fall into the ditch?

The disciple is not above his master, but whosoever will be a perfect disciple shall be as his master is.

And why seest thou a mote in thy brother's eye, but considerest not the beam that is in thine own eye?

Either, how canst thou say to thy brother: Brother, let me pull out the mote that is in thine eye, when thou seest not the beam that is in thine own eye? Thou hypocrite, cast the beam out of thine own eye first, and then shalt thou see perfectly to pull out the mote that is in thy brother's eye.

The relevance of this to the whole fabric of *Measure for Measure*, even down to the play's title, is self-evident. The Sermon on the Mount is, in effect, one of Shakespeare's main sources, and he uses it, together with other passages from the Gospels, to enrich and illuminate moral attitudes which were already present in *Promos and Cassandra* but which, judging from the frequency with which they are invoked in other plays, were substantially those to which he himself subscribed. What seems to emerge, when the various sources of inspiration are duly weighed, is that both the political and the personal morality of *Measure for Measure* are basically, though endorsed and vastly amplified, those of Whetstone's play, and that the dramatic pattern, too, is derivative.

This does not mean that new Shakespeare is but old Whetstone writ large. It was long ago remarked by James Anthony Froude that Shakespeare's distinctive excellence lies in the fact that 'his stories are not put together and his characters are not conceived to illustrate any particular law or principle' and that 'he builds his fabrics as nature does, on right and wrong; but he does not struggle to make nature more systematic than she is'. *Measure for Measure* may seem to be an exception, since it is patently intended to illustrate many of the cardinal principles of Christian teaching. Yet, unlike the orthodox Morality play, it avoids systematization, and, though it invokes a pattern of comedy current at a time when it was held to be the function of both poetry and drama to delight, which they seldom did, and to instruct, which they did only too readily, it fuses that pattern with other conceptions, some of which hark back to Shakespeare's earlier practice and are virtually exclusive to him.

*

Shakespearian tragedy, either by accident or design, conforms readily with what have come to be regarded as Aristotle's precepts as codified in the *Poetics*. It shows how men of outstanding quality are brought to ruin by a proneness to error (*hamartia*), which is not necessarily a moral flaw; how the tragic hero, in the face of his afflictions, displays a certain extravagance or exaltation of spirit (*hubris*); and how his misfortunes are presented in such a way that they lead to a *catharsis* that is 'of power by raising pity and fear, or terror, to purge the mind of those and such like passions'. Comedy in general cannot be covered by any such comprehensive formula, but Shakespearian practice, at least from *The Merchant of Venice* to *Twelfth Night*, suggests that it was responsive to something roughly analogous to this theory of tragedy. Shakespearian comedy over this period is grounded on the human circumstance that 'Journeys end in lovers meeting', and the hero, after fluctuations of fortune that resemble the reversals and discoveries of tragedy, achieves the happiness of marriage. But young people in love are desperately vulnerable (*hamartia*) and oddly pretentious (*hubris*). In all that they do they are, at one and the same time, poignantly beautiful and absurdly naïve. They provoke sympathy and ridicule in the way that the tragic hero provokes pity and terror. They proceed to a resolution which purges the mind of those and such like passions. We are shown the processes whereby immature men and women develop into people ripe for the responsibilities of marriage, so that they end by being wiser and basically more moral.

Vincentio may seem a far cry from Benedick, and Isabella an even further cry from Beatrice, yet the difference is not one of kind but of degree. In so far as it ends with the union between its two principal characters, not to mention the other impending nuptials, *Measure for Measure* is a romantic comedy, though its working out as such, owing to the plot and comic pattern derived from *Promos and Cassandra*, is revealed only spasmodically. Its villain is

> *a man whose blood*
> *Is very snow-broth one who never feels*
> *The wanton stings and motions of the sense,*
> *But doth rebate and blunt his natural edge*
> *With profits of the mind, study, and fast ...*

but it is the hero who, in I.3, bids Friar Thomas:

> *Believe not that the dribbling dart of love*
> *Can pierce a complete bosom.*

Angelo's attitude may be governed by 'a due sincerity', but Vincentio merely deludes himself with a pretentiousness that recalls Benedick's declaration, 'I will live a bachelor.' The issue of the final Act clearly shows that Cupid's dribbling dart has, after all, pierced that complete bosom. Precisely when this occurs is not made clear, but it is not unreasonable to suppose that the motion which much imports Isabella's good takes shape in IV.1 when, after the Duke has enunciated certain newly acquired wisdom about the principles of justice, the introduction of Mariana removes the monstrous threat to

Isabella, and the whole character of the play grows subtly romantic.

Isabella herself, viewed as part of a Whetstonian moral pattern, is effective as a symbol of virtue and chastity, but in the context of comedy her deficiencies are serious enough. The fact that she conveniently abjures the spiritual life when Vincentio proposes marriage need not cause us any concern, for novices, in Elizabethan comedy, were evidently allowed to change their minds as a matter of convenience. Here Shakespeare had sufficient precedent in Robert Greene's *Friar Bacon and Friar Bungay*, where the heroine, Margaret, believing that her lover, Lacy, Earl of Lincoln, has renounced her, decides to be shorn a nun, only to find Lacy returning to claim her. She justifies her decision in becomingly sanctimonious terms and affirms:

Margaret hath made a vow which may not be revoked.

Thereupon one of Lacy's followers bids her choose:

God or Lord Lacy. Which contents you best,
To be a nun, or else Lord Lacy's wife?

Margaret's response, when confronted with this choice between sacred and profane love, is immediate and startlingly uninhibited:

The flesh is frail. My lord doth know it well,
That when he comes with his enchanting face,
Whatso'er betide, I cannot say him nay.
Off goes the habit of a maiden's heart;
And, seeing Fortune will, fair Framlingham,
And all the show of holy nuns, farewell.
Lacy for me, if he will be my lord.

In the light of this Isabella's discreet and indeed tacit change of heart is a comparatively venial offence.

Her refusal to save Claudio by submitting to Angelo's

demands seems to have offended many readers, some of whom contend that she should willingly have sacrificed her virginity, and yet condemn the bed-trick, by which she escapes violation, as distasteful. This is having it both ways with a vengeance, and neither argument is valid. We have to bear in mind that, at least in the first half of the play, Isabella is very much a novice of the Order of Saint Clare, and that, although she has made no binding vows, she is, by choice, subject to the disciplines of an order that imposes chastity upon its members. To comply with Angelo's proposal would be to commit deadly sin. There is no escape from this, any more than there is from the belief prevalent at the time that the punishment for deadly sin was eternal damnation. If we remind ourselves that hundreds of the Tudor martyrs attainted of heresy submitted uncomplainingly to a terrible death in the belief that it is better to burn for an hour or so on earth than to burn in Hell throughout all eternity, we shall better understand Isabella's motive in refusing to commit mortal sin, and, if any doubt then remains in our minds, we may further remind ourselves of the uncompromising doctrine of the Roman Catholic church to which she belongs. It may be pertinent here, in order to bring home to the reader that this doctrine, unlike the notion of hell-fire, is not a thing which belongs to a less enlightened age, to cite the unequivocal pronouncement of a saintly and humane Victorian, Cardinal Newman:

'The Catholic Church holds that it were better for sun and moon to drop from heaven, for the earth to fail, and for all the many millions who are upon it to die of starvation in extremest agony as far as temporal affliction goes, than that one soul, I will not say should be lost, but should (even) commit one venial sin.'

In the light of this doctrine, the comparatively mild temporal affliction entailed in Claudio's execution will, I think, appear in its proper perspective.

The basic flaw in Isabella's character – as the heroine in a romantic comedy, that is – lies in other things. If Vincentio has something of the pretentiousness of Benedick, she exhibits more than a little of the shrewishness of Beatrice. Her rejection of Claudio's plea is, I have suggested, both valid and inevitable, but that does not seem to justify the storm of abuse which she unleashes in III.1.139–54. Such vituperation is really the outcome of what is, in the early stages of the play, an excess of piety – even more extreme than Angelo's – which arises out of a false set of values. Just how excessive those values are emerges in her conversation with Francisca at the beginning of I.4. When she asks,

> And have you nuns no farther privileges?

Francisca rejoins,

> Are not these large enough?

and Isabella's response is startling:

> Yes, truly. I speak not as desiring more,
> But rather wishing a more strict restraint
> Upon the sisterhood, the votarists of Saint Clare.

When it is borne in mind that the Order of Saint Clare, with its insistence on seclusion, penitence, and extreme poverty, was from its inauguration one of the most austere of the religious orders, and that its subsequent tendency was towards augmented austerity of life, it becomes clear that, unless Shakespeare was entirely ignorant of these facts (which he almost certainly was not), Isabella is setting up to be more Catholic than the Pope – not to mention Saint Francis and Saint Clare. She is guilty of presumption, certainly, and a presumption which comes perilously near to being the sin of pride.

There is a confusion of values, too, in her attitude to her brother's transgression. His fault is to have anticipated marriage with one who, in his own words,

> is fast my wife
> Save that we do denunciation lack
> Of outward order.

It is highly unlikely that Shakespeare's own attitude was one of censure in view of the fact that his daughter Susanna was born six months after his marriage to Anne Hathaway, and, considering the common Elizabethan practice of *sponsalia de praesenti*, whereby vows exchanged in the presence of a witness, though subject to consecration at a later date, were held to constitute full marriage, it is more than doubtful whether Claudio's offence can reasonably be regarded as an offence at all. Yet Isabella complacently begins her plea to Angelo at II.2.29–33 with:

> There is a vice that most I do abhor,
> And most desire should meet the blow of justice,
> For which I would not plead, but that I must,
> For which I must not plead, but that I am
> At war 'twixt will and will not . . .

and later, at II.4.69–73, we find her prepared to admit that it may be sin either for her to plead or for Angelo to grant. If Claudio's slip (or, indeed, premarital intercourse in any degree) is the vice that she most abhors, she must surely stand convicted of a gross ineptitude in moral judgement. The Church's teaching on illicit sexual intercourse is unequivocal, but it is questionable whether any creed in any age has regarded this as the most abhorrent of all sins. The account given in Saint John 8.3–11 of the woman taken in adultery – a passage which colours the attitudes assumed elsewhere in *Measure for Measure* – establishes Christ's own readiness to pronounce complete absolution for such misdemeanours:

> *And the Scribes and Pharisees brought unto Him a woman taken in adultery, and when they had set her down in the midst,*
>
> *They said unto Him: Master, this woman was taken in adultery, even as the deed was a-doing.*
>
> *Moses in the law commanded us that such should be stoned, but what sayest Thou?*
>
> *This they said to tempt Him, that they might accuse Him. But Jesus stooped down, and with His finger wrote on the ground.*
>
> *So, when they continued asking Him, He lift up Himself and said unto them: Let him that is among you without sin cast the first stone at her.*
>
> *And again He stooped down, and wrote on the ground.*
>
> *And when they heard this, being accused of their own consciences, they went out one by one, beginning at the eldest, even unto the last. And Jesus was left alone, and the woman standing in the midst.*
>
> *When Jesus had lift Himself up, and saw no man but the woman, He said unto her: Woman, where are those thine accusers? Hath no man condemned thee?*
>
> *She said, No man, Lord. And Jesus said, Neither do I condemn thee: Go, and sin no more.*

The irony is that Isabella, in the two speeches mentioned reveals herself as innocently subscribing to the same distorted values as Angelo, who, at II.4.42–9, actually declares that there is as much justification for condoning murder as there is for countenancing

> *Their saucy sweetness that do coin God's image*
> *In stamps that are forbid.*

33

Isabella, like the Duke, thus begins as a character deeply flawed who eventually learns wisdom and charity. The stages in her development are subtle and gradual, but it may be suggested that the change in her attitudes is approximately coincident with that in Vincentio's. Her acceptance of the bed-trick at III.1.260 symbolizes a reversal of her previous values and marks a new access of human understanding.

In thus learning to know each other, to know themselves and their fellow-men, in shedding pretentiousness and false values, and in resolving themselves from discordant twain to concordant one, Vincentio and Isabella conform to what we take to be the normal pattern of Shakespearian romantic comedy. That pattern, though at times obscured by the powerful moral element in the play, is reinforced by the story of the wronged Mariana, whose misfortunes issue from happenings – the miscarriage at sea of her brother Frederick – which are related evocatively in III.1.201–44, and recall both in matter and manner the hazards of the preceding comedies. In IV.1 we are transported to the world of romance itself – to the moated grange, to Mariana and her music, to the lyrical description of Angelo's garden, and to kindly intrigue – in short, to a world as far removed from the corrupt atmosphere of Vienna as Portia's enchanted Belmont is from the commercial turmoil of Venice.

*

The complex figure of Angelo fits as conveniently into the scheme of romantic comedy as into the moral and political pattern, but I believe that in the main he belongs to another concept of comedy, deriving from the satirical genre that was in vogue at about the time when *Measure for Measure* was written. In plays of this kind the vices and follies of mankind were whipped (as the *mastix* element in

such titles as *Satiromastix* and *Histriomastix* implies),
anatomized, and purged, and the offending characters un-
trussed or exposed. Marston and Dekker did much to
promote this comedy of exposure, but it was Ben Jonson
who gave classic shape to their ideas and impulses and
established a 'comedy of humours' which later yielded
such masterpieces as *Volpone* and *The Alchemist*. Shakespeare seems not to have made any serious attempt to con-
tribute to a dramatic kind that was alien to his genius and
probably little to his liking, but that does not mean that
he was wholly unresponsive to the new patterns, and such
creations as Angelo suggest that he was prepared to go
some way with Jonson but no further.

Already by 1600, in the induction to *Every Man out of
his Humour*, Jonson had clearly enunciated his conception
of a 'humour':

> *So in every human body,*
> *The choler, melancholy, phlegm, and blood,*
> *By reason that they flow continually*
> *In some one part, and are not continent,*
> *Receive the name of humours. Now thus far*
> *It may, by metaphor, apply itself*
> *Unto the general disposition:*
> *As when some one peculiar quality*
> *Doth so possess a man, that it doth draw*
> *All his affects, his spirits, and his powers,*
> *In their confluctions, all to run one way,*
> *This may be truly said to be a humour.*
> *But that a rook, by wearing a pied feather,*
> *The cable hat-band, or the three-piled ruff,*
> *A yard of shoe-tie, or the Switzer's knot*
> *On his French garters, should affect a humour –*
> *O, it is more than most ridiculous.*

35

After this exposition, he proclaims that the purpose of his play is to 'scourge those apes', and to anatomize 'the time's deformity'. Shakespeare's presentation of Angelo seems to follow these patterns and to illustrate, in the process, some of those problems which confronted Jonson himself – especially the difficult one of balancing realism with the kind of excess which results from the operations of a dominant humour. There are occasions when Angelo is very much a human being, and all too real. As

> man, proud man,
> *Dressed in a little brief authority* . . .
> (II.2.117–18)

he demonstrates the lesson so often taught by history: that power corrupts. He finds, as others who have aspired to sanctity have found, that he is, after all, susceptible to

> *The wanton stings and motions of the sense* . . .

and the discovery appals him. Even more terrifying is the recognition that the temptation to deflower a virgin, half-committed to vows of chastity, is one which he is unable to resist. His remorse of conscience, powerfully depicted in II.2 and II.4, is anguished and moving, though we may remind ourselves that his designs on Isabella are governed by what are substantially the reasons for Iago's assault on Michael Cassio (*Othello*, V.1.19–20):

> *He hath a daily beauty in his life*
> *That makes me ugly*

and that his sense of guilt lies no deeper than that of Claudius in *Hamlet*. Yet the human traits, some more apparent than real, appear only intermittently, and it is a curiously stylized villain who emerges in the actual dénouement. If Isabella pleads (V.1.442–4):

> *I partly think*
> *A due sincerity governèd his deeds*
> *Till he did look on me*

this is surely a plea imposed by the needs of both Christian charity and romantic comedy, and the same is true of Mariana's almost incredible affirmation (V.1.422–3):

> *O my dear lord,*
> *I crave no other, nor no better man.*

For Angelo himself has now been reduced to little more than a puppet or a motion generative, who frankly admits his guilt, craves 'Immediate sentence' and 'sequent death', and finally, by 'a quickening in his eye', 'perceives he's safe'. There is strangely little of that repentance which both the moral and the romantic aspects of the play would seem to demand, and this, I suggest, is because Shakespeare conceived of him primarily as a 'humours' character, dominated by a sham Puritanism, who has been finally exposed and humiliated.

Puritans had long been regarded as fair game by the dramatists, and not without cause. Just as the followers of Wycliffe had earlier denounced the performing of Miracle plays, so their successors in the sixteenth century indiscriminately condemned poets and dramatists as 'fathers of lies, pipes of vanity, and schools of abuse', and though these charges, levelled by Stephen Gosson in his notorious *School of Abuse* in 1579, were promptly and brilliantly rebutted by Philip Sidney in *The Defence of Poesy*, the opposition continued unabated, with the result that public play-acting was permanently banned in the Puritan-dominated City of London, and the dramatists and their companies were forced to operate in Southwark, where theatres sprang up adjacent to the bear-garden and the brothels in an atmosphere that must closely have resembled that of Vienna in *Measure for Measure*.

Hence precisian and playwright were at perpetual war, and, though Shakespeare's tolerant nature probably accorded a degree of 'due sincerity' to the Puritans of his day, their extreme rigidity and sanctimoniousness made them a fair target. The assumption that one automatically belongs to the Lord's elect is presumptuous and self-deluding, and can all too easily degenerate into hypocrisy. And Angelo's character, whatever its other obscurities or complexities, affords a fairly clear pattern of self-deception not wholly free from hypocrisy's taint.

There seems little doubt that one of Duke Vincentio's intentions, from the outset, is to place Angelo in a position which allows this excess or dominant humour to be fully exhibited and exposed. Early in the play (I.3.12) the Duke describes his deputy as

> *A man of stricture and firm abstinence* ...

and a little later he enlarges on this:

> *Lord Angelo is precise,*
> *Stands at a guard with envy, scarce confesses*
> *That his blood flows, or that his appetite*
> *Is more to bread than stone.*

There is nothing to suggest that he regards these as virtuous qualities. On the contrary the lines with which the second of these speeches closes:

> *Hence shall we see,*
> *If power change purpose, what our seemers be*

offer a clear indication that the Duke already knows Angelo to be a dissembler, and the revelations in III.1 about his treatment of Mariana, which can scarcely rest on freshly acquired knowledge, establish that this is so. Dissimulation, then, is, from the very beginning, Angelo's revealed 'humour', and the things that Vincentio does not already know are those which become the essence of the whole comedy – that the dissembler will turn tyrant, will attempt to despoil Isabella, and will, in order to save his own reputation, seek to carry out his original sentence on Claudio. In short, Angelo is a notable example of how 'some one peculiar quality' can possess a man, and both presentation and excoriation conform substantially to Jonsonian precept and practice.

*

The complex pattern of plot and motive in *Measure for Measure* is powerfully reinforced with the low-life elements familiar enough in Shakespeare's earlier comedies, and it may here be helpful to cite Dr Johnson's general comment:

> *Of this play the light or comic part is very natural and pleasing, but the grave scenes, if a few passages be excepted, have more labour than elegance. The plot is rather intricate than artful.*

It signifies little that Johnson, who was ignorant of the immediate sources of *Measure for Measure*, should have failed to recognize the particular virtues of the play's intricacy, or that he should have taken an unnecessarily lukewarm view of the serious scenes, save for 'a few passages' which are doubtless those which expound a morality congenial to the author of *The Vanity of Human Wishes*. The important detail is that he responded, as more than a few later critics have failed to do, to the vitality of 'the light or comic part' – that is, to the scenes which involve such stock Shakespearian grotesques as Elbow,

Pompey, and Mistress Overdone. More significant still is his implicit recognition of the distinctive contributions of Barnardine and Lucio. Both make a greater impact on the stage, where their capacity for seizing the initiative emerges clearly, than in the study. Both, in the general context of the play, are the ultimate rebarbative products of the Duke's years of misrule. Nevertheless they are made representatives of a species of truth which Vincentio has hitherto refused to face. Lucio, who, in production, can easily steal much of the limelight, is one of Shakespeare's great paradoxical characters. He speaks scarcely one word true throughout the whole play, and yet his lies and distortions shape themselves into a kind of truth. It is through him, as much as anyone, that the Duke, who, 'above all other strifes, contended especially to know himself', advances decisively towards that self-knowledge which both the romantic and the moral fabric of the play require.

*

The style of *Measure for Measure* is skilfully shaped to suit material that, by its very nature, offers little scope for lyricism or sustained flights of the imagination. There are speeches – by Isabella in II.2.57–66, by Vincentio in III.1.5–41, by Claudio in III.1.121–35 – that surprise by a fine excess, but the writing is, for the greater part, carefully and very properly controlled. If the play lacks the rich patterns of imagery that we normally associate with Shakespeare, it is because the dramatist had other things to offer. In *Measure for Measure* the sheer brilliance of presentation creates its own illusion which leads us to imagine that far more is happening than actually does happen. Executions, rape, and all the attendant circumstances are planned for a tomorrow that never seems to

come, so that for most of the time we are in a world of
ideas and purposes. This is made apparent at the end by
Isabella in her defence of Angelo:

> *His act did not o'ertake his bad intent,*
> *And must be buried but as an intent*
> *That perished by the way. Thoughts are no subjects,*
> *Intents but merely thoughts.*　　　　V.1.448–51

Hence, in a play that is concerned less with action than
with the principles of action, Shakespeare tends to substitute ideas for images. It has been recognized that *Measure
for Measure* makes extensive use of certain key-words:
authority, mercy, grace, scope, liberty, restraint, justice.
Since abstraction often begets abstraction, it is not sur-
prising that, as we proceed through the play, we meet a
striking array of abstract nouns that Shakespeare does not
use elsewhere – *morality, denunciation, propagation,
approbation, infliction, renouncement, remissness, uncleanness, austereness, prompture, advisings, doubleness, inequality, confutation*. There is, of course, no dearth of
concrete images, many of them memorable, but it is not
readily apparent that Shakespeare attempted to organize
those images into functional patterns such as occur in
The Merchant of Venice, Macbeth, or *Antony and Cleopatra*.

It is perhaps because *Measure for Measure* is so much a
play of ideas that irony emerges as one of its most notable
features. Like the tragedies, and unlike most of the
comedies, it is infused with elements of duality, contradiction, indecision, vulnerability, error, and coinci-
dence which come near to giving the impression that
action and character are at times affected by the workings
of a blind destiny. The presentation is so complex and the
overtones are so subtle and numerous that a total audit is
virtually impossible and it must here suffice merely to

indicate those circumstances which are, in themselves, ironic and promotive of irony. There is, at the outset, the implied discrepancy between the Duke's virtuous and politic nature and the defective pattern of government for which his misguided notion of mercy is directly answerable, and, arising from this, the paradox that he is shown to be a wiser governor after he has temporarily renounced the right to govern. If, at this stage, he is led to doubt the validity of Angelo's code, it is substantially because Isabella's example disposes him towards sweet reasonableness. Yet there is a corresponding irony in the agent of goodness and mercy. Her very virtue is made responsible for the temptations and sufferings of others. Angelo's icy rectitude is corrupted by her purity and innocence, and Claudio's miseries are intensified by an outburst of vituperation that shocks and perplexes. The last words that she speaks to her brother in the play (III.1.154) are

'Tis best that thou diest quickly . . .

and he is left pleading to be heard. The exchanges between them are heavy with contradiction and paradox. We may ask whether it is sheer cowardice which leads a man lawfully condemned to ask his sister to submit to something which, with divine warrant, she fears as acutely as he fears death. The issue is complicated by the fact that Claudio, deluded by the supposed wisdom of Angelo, is half convinced that such submission would not be a capital sin. Isabella's refusal is, for reasons already specified, necessary to the religious context, yet her failure to allow for human frailty is disturbing. What Claudio's temporary lapse exemplifies is that, though the spirit is willing, the flesh is weak. His sister's response falls short of the Christian ideal. It is reasonable that she should give vent to righteous indignation, but, in the event, that virtue comes dangerously near to the deadly sin of wrath, prompted by the still deadlier one of spiritual pride.

Angelo is a living paradox compounded of many ironies. The maintenance of law has been committed to him yet he proves vulnerable to the temptations that his seemingly sincere but inflexible outlook condemns in others. From the contemplation of an offence far more heinous than that of Claudio he declines still further to the moral level of Barnardine and, like him, presumes to set himself above the law. The same kind of presumption extends to other characters. Isabella aspires to a perfection greater than the Church prescribes and the Duke, with his immunity to 'the dribbling dart of love', transgresses natural law. This excess reaches its climax when, at their joint instigation, Mariana is made the substitute for Isabella. The device has aroused misgivings in many critics, though it is clearly necessary that the union between Angelo and Mariana should be finally affirmed in order not only to resolve their personal difficulties but also to secure the redemption of Angelo. The absolute ethical justification is less easy to establish. The essence of Vincentio's assurance at IV.1.71–4:

> *He is your husband on a pre-contract.*
> *To bring you thus together, 'tis no sin,*
> *Sith that the justice of your title to him*
> *Doth flourish the deceit . . .*

is that of the end justifying the means, and, as such, could be made the basis of interminable debate. It is better, therefore, to suspend judgement and to accept the stratagem as a genuine, but unusual, element of comedy which the present-day reader may wish to designate 'sick humour' – a term which would presumably relieve it of immorality without detracting from its irony. The subterfuge, employed by ordinary mortals, and perhaps with less exalted motives, might well escape comment. But it is ironic that a duke, God's deputy, and a novice, dedicated to unworldly things, should practise a procurer's trick. The irony of Angelo's situation is palpable. In committing an act of lust he unwittingly performs an act that is pardonable in the light of subsequent events, and is granted the means of salvation through what, in his heart, he believes to be mortal sin. In the process that sin is avoided but he now stands convicted of precisely the same offence as that for which he has condemned Claudio to death.

Irony attaching to plot and character is given its most powerful expression in the dénouement when the Duke, in his friar's gown, and Isabella, in her novice's habit, dissociate themselves from the particular obligations which those habiliments symbolize and belatedly emerge as hero and heroine of a romantic comedy. The curious thing is that the transformation renders them wiser and essentially holier persons. Lucio's '*Cucullus non facit monachum*' shows itself to be a truth in a sense far deeper than his superficial worldly wisdom could ever have apprehended.

But the matter does not end here. There is, we may say, an overall irony of presentation in that themes so strenuous and painful that they lie outside the normal scope of comedy are nevertheless resolved, with a virtuosity that defies analysis, in terms of romantic comedy. Stretching beyond this, there is a species of moral irony peculiar to *Measure for Measure*. The precept: 'Judge not, and ye shall not be judged: condemn not, and ye shall not be condemned: forgive, and ye shall be forgiven' is one that Shakespeare evidently intended the members of his audience to lay to their own hearts. He does not himself pronounce judgement on his creatures and, in this play, he effectively conveys that it would be presumptuous for us to attempt to do so. We comply, though it is not without effort that we forgive Angelo. The ultimate irony is that, for many of us, it requires a still greater effort to forgive Isabella's treatment of her brother.

*

All in all *Measure for Measure* emerges as a play of a rather unusual kind. Swinburne's description of it as a 'great indefinable poem or unclassifiable play' seems applicable in senses other than those which he perhaps intended. For, its greatness conceded, the exact position of *Measure for Measure* in the Shakespeare hierarchy remains unsettled, and its present-day encomiasts are not necessarily wiser than Johnson and Coleridge, both of whom were sensitive to its defects. It may be said, without disparagement, that this play fails to rank among Shakespeare's supremely great achievements. The dramatist does not quite succeed in the virtually impossible task of unifying several patterns of comedy, and, in this particular, Dr Johnson's apparent misgivings may simply testify to the profundity of his insight. It is just to remark that, save for the passing glimpse of Mariana in her moated grange, the play fails to transport us into the enchanted world of Belmont, Arden, or Illyria. And if, like Keats, 'we hate poetry that has a palpable design upon us', we may resent the insistent morality that seems to take the place of such enchantment. These are admissible charges but it would be foolish to press them too hard. If Shakespeare, for the occasion, was more virtuous than was his wont, he was careful not to deprive us of cakes and ale. *Measure for Measure* lacks none of the vitality of *Much Ado About Nothing* or *As You Like It* but, with its more searching inquiries into man's potential for good and evil and its definition of his duty towards his fellows, it carries comedy into a new dimension. Shakespeare has here advanced towards the questions posed by the great tragedies and adumbrated the answers given in the final romances.

FURTHER READING

Editions

THE new Arden *Measure for Measure* (1965), edited by J. W. Lever, provides a long, yet concentrated, introduction which discusses text, date, and sources and proceeds to an impressive account of the play's form and themes. Other editions include those by Arthur Quiller-Couch and J. Dover Wilson (New Cambridge, 1922), W. H. Durham (Yale, 1926), R. C. Bald (Pelican, 1956), and S. Nagarajan (Signet, 1964). Ernst Leisi's *Measure for Measure* (Heidelberg, 1964) is styled 'An Old-Spelling and Old-Meaning Edition' and is of particular value for its close examination of the ascertainable semantic range of individual words.

Sources

George Whetstone's *Promos and Cassandra* (1578), the primary source of *Measure for Measure*, is reprinted in the second volume of Geoffrey Bullough's *Narrative and Dramatic Sources of Shakespeare* (1958), together with the narrative version from Cinthio's *Hecatommithi* (1565) and his dramatized version, *Epitia* (1583). Bullough prints several analogues, but omits Whetstone's prose account in his *Heptameron of Civil Discourses*, which is, however, readily accessible in T. J. B. Spencer's attractive *Elizabethan Love Stories* (Penguin Shakespeare Library, 1968). The bases of Shakespeare's religious and political thought in the play are effectively discussed in Elizabeth M. Pope's 'The Renaissance Background of *Measure for Measure*' (*Shakespeare Survey 2*, 1949). David Lloyd Stevenson includes a revision of his 1959 essay on Shakespeare's possible obligations to James I's *Basilicon Doron* in *The Achievement of Shakespeare's 'Measure for Measure'* (1966).

47

Criticism

Early criticism of *Measure for Measure* is scanty. Dr Johnson's comments are mentioned in the introduction to the present edition, and it will suffice to remark that Dryden (*An Essay of Dramatic Poesy*, 1668) dismissed the play as 'meanly written' and that Coleridge thought it 'a hateful work'. There are discussions of varying quality in Hazlitt's *The Characters of Shakespeare's Plays* (1817) and Swinburne's *A Study of Shakespeare* (1880), but the first audit likely to engage the sympathy of the modern reader is the 'appreciation' by Walter Pater (*Works, V,* 1901; reprinted in *Shakespeare's Later Comedies*, edited by D. J. Palmer, Penguin Shakespeare Library, 1971).

John Masefield (*William Shakespeare*, 1911) made the important and revolutionary claim that *Measure for Measure* is one of Shakespeare's supreme masterpieces and Angelo one of his best-drawn characters. A similar enthusiasm is displayed in F. R. Leavis's 'The Greatness of *Measure for Measure*' (*Scrutiny*, 1942; reprinted in *The Common Pursuit*) and D. L. Stevenson's *The Achievement of Shakespeare's 'Measure for Measure'* (1966).

In his introduction to the New Cambridge *Measure for Measure* (1922), an unsatisfactory but, for years, highly influential edition, Quiller-Couch posed the question: what is wrong with this play? Nearly all the books and articles that have appeared since that time are, in some form or other, attempts to supply an answer, or rather a bewildering number of answers. It is possible here to mention only a selection of what is offered and to indicate the general trends of such criticism.

C. J. Sisson's 1934 British Academy lecture, *The Mythical Sorrows of Shakespeare*, though not directly concerned with *Measure for Measure*, is highly relevant to the dramatist's outlook at the time when the play was written. Sisson's contention that the Shakespeare of 1603–4 was anything but a pessimist is developed in R. W. Chambers's lecture *The Jacobean Shakespeare and 'Measure for Measure'* (British Academy, 1937), later expanded and given classic form in the two essays, 'The Elizabethan and the Jacobean Shakespeare' and 'Measure for Measure', printed in *Man's Unconquerable Mind* (1939).

One school of criticism sees *Measure for Measure* as one of a number of plays, somewhat arbitrarily determined, which are concerned with moral problems that either troubled the dramatist personally or commended themselves to him as central principles to a dramatic action. Discussions of the play under this head are furnished by W. W. Lawrence, *Shakespeare's Problem Comedies* (1931; Penguin Shakespeare Library, 1969), E. M. W. Tillyard, *Shakespeare's Problem Plays* (1949), and Ernest Schanzer, *The Problem Plays of Shakespeare* (1963; reprinted in *Shakespeare's Later Comedies*). The play's ponderable religious content has caused it to be interpreted as a dramatic parable by G. Wilson Knight in '*Measure for Measure* and the Gospels' (*The Wheel of Fire*, 1930), by R. W. Battenhouse in '*Measure for Measure* and the Christian Doctrine of Atonement' (*Publications of the Modern Language Association of America*, 1946), and, more temperately, by Nevill Coghill in 'Comic Form in *Measure for Measure*' (*Shakespeare Survey 8*, 1955). Josephine Waters Bennett's '*Measure for Measure' as Royal Entertainment* (1966) treats the religious themes as specifically Nativity ones and relates the play to the Christmas entertainment of James I. She places more emphasis than has hitherto been usual upon the impact of the play as pure comedy. The same tendency is apparent in D. L. Stevenson's *The Achievement of Shakespeare's 'Measure for Measure'* (1966), which also challenges received opinion by divesting the play of all religious significance.

An earlier book, Mary Lascelles's *Shakespeare's 'Measure for Measure'* (1953), essays the difficult task of presenting the play as a unity but might perhaps better serve as a general commentary which offers shrewd judgements on sources, text, characterization, and dramatic effect. An extract is reprinted in *Shakespeare's Later Comedies*. Articles which throw light on particular aspects of the play include M. C. Bradbrook's 'Authority, Truth and Justice in *Measure for Measure*' (*Review of English Studies*, 1941), W. M. T. Dodds's 'The Character of Angelo in *Measure for Measure*' (*Modern Language Review*, 1946), William Empson's ' "Sense" in *Measure for Measure*' (in *The Structure of Complex Words*, 1951), and Ernest Schanzer's 'The Marriage Contracts in *Measure for Measure*' (*Shakespeare Survey 13*, 1960). There is a stimulating chapter on the play in Harriett Hawkins's *Likenesses of Truth in Elizabethan and Restoration Drama* (1972).

A useful conspectus of the divergent views about the play is provided by R. M. Smith in 'Interpretations of *Measure for Measure*' (*Shakespeare Quarterly*, 1950), though, as will be evident, much has happened, including three books devoted exclusively to the play, since the article appeared. If the reader finds the diversity of interpretation perplexing, he can draw comfort from Clifford Leech's 'The "Meaning" of *Measure for Measure*' (*Shakespeare Survey 3*, 1950) which accepts the play as a complex organism and warns us against relying on any one exegesis. Those who wish to know something of the impact of *Measure for Measure* as a stage piece will find little to enlighten them in the literature about the play but are well served by Richard David's 'Shakespeare's Comedies and the Modern Stage' (*Shakespeare Survey 4*, 1951) which considers production problems with special reference to *Love's Labour's Lost* and *Measure for Measure*.

What were Mariana's feelings after she had been deserted by Angelo? The question was posed not, as might be thought, by A. C. Bradley, but by Tennyson, who supplied the answer in *Mariana*. This lyric shows how one great poet can respond to the merest promptings of another in a way that beggars the best endeavours of all critics.

MEASURE FOR MEASURE

THE CHARACTERS IN THE PLAY

Vincentio, the DUKE
ANGELO, the Deputy
ESCALUS, an ancient Lord
CLAUDIO, a young Gentleman
LUCIO, a Fantastic
Two other like Gentlemen
PROVOST
FRIAR THOMAS
FRIAR PETER
ELBOW, a simple Constable
FROTH, a foolish Gentleman
POMPEY, a Clown, servant to Mistress Overdone
ABHORSON, an Executioner
BARNARDINE, a dissolute Prisoner
JUSTICE
VARRIUS, a friend to the Duke
ISABELLA, a sister to Claudio
MARIANA, betrothed to Angelo
JULIET, beloved of Claudio
FRANCISCA, a Nun
MISTRESS OVERDONE, a Bawd

Lords and Attendants
Officers
Citizens
A Prisoner
A Boy
A Messenger

DUKE
  Escalus.
ESCALUS
  My lord.
DUKE
  Of government the properties to unfold
  Would seem in me t'affect speech and discourse,
  Since I am put to know that your own science
  Exceeds, in that, the lists of all advice
  My strength can give you. Then no more remains
  But that, to your sufficiency, as your worth is able,
  And let them work. The nature of our people,
  Our city's institutions, and the terms   10
  For common justice, y'are as pregnant in
  As art and practice hath enrichèd any
  That we remember. There is our commission,
  From which we would not have you warp. Call hither,
  I say, bid come before us Angelo.   *Exit an Attendant*
  What figure of us think you he will bear?
  For you must know, we have with special soul
  Elected him our absence to supply,
  Lent him our terror, dressed him with our love,
  And given his deputation all the organs   20
  Of our own power. What think you of it?
ESCALUS
  If any in Vienna be of worth
  To undergo such ample grace and honour,

It is Lord Angelo.

Enter Angelo

DUKE   Look where he comes.

ANGELO

Always obedient to your grace's will,
I come to know your pleasure.

DUKE   Angelo,
There is a kind of character in thy life
That to th'observer doth thy history
Fully unfold. Thyself and thy belongings
30 Are not thine own so proper as to waste
Thyself upon thy virtues, they on thee.
Heaven doth with us as we with torches do,
Not light them for themselves: for if our virtues
Did not go forth of us, 'twere all alike
As if we had them not. Spirits are not finely touched
But to fine issues, nor Nature never lends
The smallest scruple of her excellence
But, like a thrifty goddess, she determines
Herself the glory of a creditor,
40 Both thanks and use. But I do bend my speech
To one that can my part in him advertise.
Hold therefore, Angelo:
In our remove be thou at full ourself.
Mortality and mercy in Vienna
Live in thy tongue and heart. Old Escalus,
Though first in question, is thy secondary.
Take thy commission.

ANGELO   Now, good my lord,
Let there be some more test made of my metal
Before so noble and so great a figure
50 Be stamped upon't.

DUKE   No more evasion.
We have with leavened and preparèd choice

Proceeded to you; therefore take your honours.
Our haste from hence is of so quick condition
That it prefers itself, and leaves unquestioned
Matters of needful value. We shall write to you,
As time and our concernings shall importune,
How it goes with us, and do look to know
What doth befall you here. So fare you well.
To th'hopeful execution do I leave you
Of your commissions.

ANGELO   Yet give leave, my lord,   60
That we may bring you something on the way.

DUKE
My haste may not admit it;
Nor need you, on mine honour, have to do
With any scruple. Your scope is as mine own,
So to enforce or qualify the laws
As to your soul seems good. Give me your hand.
I'll privily away: I love the people,
But do not like to stage me to their eyes;
Though it do well, I do not relish well
Their loud applause and aves vehement,   70
Nor do I think the man of safe discretion
That does affect it. Once more, fare you well.

ANGELO
The heavens give safety to your purposes!

ESCALUS
Lead forth and bring you back in happiness!

DUKE
I thank you. Fare you well.   *Exit*

ESCALUS
I shall desire you, sir, to give me leave
To have free speech with you, and it concerns me
To look into the bottom of my place.
A power I have, but of what strength and nature

80 I am not yet instructed.

ANGELO

'Tis so with me. Let us withdraw together,
And we may soon our satisfaction have
Touching that point.

ESCALUS   I'll wait upon your honour. *Exeunt*

I.2   *Enter Lucio and two other Gentlemen*

LUCIO If the Duke, with the other dukes, come not to
composition with the King of Hungary, why then all the
dukes fall upon the King.

FIRST GENTLEMAN Heaven grant us its peace, but not
the King of Hungary's!

SECOND GENTLEMAN Amen.

LUCIO Thou conclud'st like the sanctimonious pirate,
that went to sea with the Ten Commandments, but
scraped one out of the table.

10 SECOND GENTLEMAN 'Thou shalt not steal'?

LUCIO Ay, that he razed.

FIRST GENTLEMAN Why, 'twas a commandment to
command the captain and all the rest from their func-
tions. They put forth to steal. There's not a soldier of
us all that, in the thanksgiving before meat, do relish the
petition well that prays for peace.

SECOND GENTLEMAN I never heard any soldier dislike it.

LUCIO I believe thee, for I think thou never wast where
grace was said.

20 SECOND GENTLEMAN No? A dozen times at least.

FIRST GENTLEMAN What? In metre?

LUCIO In any proportion, or in any language.

FIRST GENTLEMAN I think, or in any religion.

LUCIO Ay, why not? Grace is grace, despite of all
controversy; as, for example, thou thyself art a wicked
villain, despite of all grace.

58

FIRST GENTLEMAN Well, there went but a pair of shears between us.

LUCIO I grant: as there may between the lists and the velvet. Thou art the list. 30

FIRST GENTLEMAN And thou the velvet. Thou art good velvet. Thou'rt a three-piled piece, I warrant thee. I had as lief be a list of an English kersey as be piled, as thou art piled, for a French velvet. Do I speak feelingly now?

LUCIO I think thou dost, and indeed with most painful feeling of thy speech. I will, out of thine own confession, learn to begin thy health, but, whilst I live, forget to drink after thee.

FIRST GENTLEMAN I think I have done myself wrong, 40 have I not?

SECOND GENTLEMAN Yes, that thou hast, whether thou art tainted or free.

Enter Mistress Overdone

LUCIO Behold, behold, where Madam Mitigation comes.

FIRST GENTLEMAN I have purchased as many diseases under her roof as come to –

SECOND GENTLEMAN To what, I pray?

LUCIO Judge.

SECOND GENTLEMAN To three thousand dolours a year.

FIRST GENTLEMAN Ay, and more. 50

LUCIO A French crown more.

FIRST GENTLEMAN Thou art always figuring diseases in me, but thou art full of error. I am sound.

LUCIO Nay, not, as one would say, healthy, but so sound as things that are hollow. Thy bones are hollow. Impiety has made a feast of thee.

FIRST GENTLEMAN How now, which of your hips has the most profound sciatica?

MISTRESS OVERDONE Well, well; there's one yonder

60 arrested and carried to prison was worth five thousand of you all.

SECOND GENTLEMAN Who's that, I pray thee?

MISTRESS OVERDONE Marry, sir, that's Claudio, Signor Claudio.

FIRST GENTLEMAN Claudio to prison? 'Tis not so.

MISTRESS OVERDONE Nay, but I know 'tis so. I saw him arrested, saw him carried away, and, which is more, within these three days his head to be chopped off.

LUCIO But, after all this fooling, I would not have it so.
70 Art thou sure of this?

MISTRESS OVERDONE I am too sure of it; and it is for getting Madam Julietta with child.

LUCIO Believe me, this may be. He promised to meet me two hours since, and he was ever precise in promise-keeping.

SECOND GENTLEMAN Besides, you know, it draws something near to the speech we had to such a purpose.

FIRST GENTLEMAN But most of all agreeing with the proclamation.

80 LUCIO Away. Let's go learn the truth of it.

Exeunt Lucio and Gentlemen

MISTRESS OVERDONE Thus, what with the war, what with the sweat, what with the gallows, and what with poverty, I am custom-shrunk.

Enter Pompey. A Gaoler and Prisoner pass over the stage

How now? What's the news with you?

POMPEY Yonder man is carried to prison.

MISTRESS OVERDONE Well, what has he done?

POMPEY A woman.

MISTRESS OVERDONE But what's his offence?

POMPEY Groping for trouts in a peculiar river.

90 MISTRESS OVERDONE What? Is there a maid with child by him?

POMPEY No, but there's a woman with maid by him. You have not heard of the proclamation, have you?

MISTRESS OVERDONE What proclamation, man?

POMPEY All houses in the suburbs of Vienna must be plucked down.

MISTRESS OVERDONE And what shall become of those in the city?

POMPEY They shall stand for seed. They had gone down too, but that a wise burgher put in for them. 100

MISTRESS OVERDONE But shall all our houses of resort in the suburbs be pulled down?

POMPEY To the ground, mistress.

MISTRESS OVERDONE Why, here's a change indeed in the commonwealth. What shall become of me?

POMPEY Come, fear not you; good counsellors lack no clients. Though you change your place, you need not change your trade. I'll be your tapster still. Courage, there will be pity taken on you. You that have worn your eyes almost out in the service, you will be considered. 110

MISTRESS OVERDONE What's to do here, Thomas Tapster? Let's withdraw.

POMPEY Here comes Signor Claudio, led by the provost to prison; and there's Madam Juliet. *Exeunt*
Enter Provost, Claudio, Juliet, Officers, Lucio, and two Gentlemen

CLAUDIO
Fellow, why dost thou show me thus to th'world?
Bear me to prison, where I am committed.

PROVOST
I do it not in evil disposition,
But from Lord Angelo by special charge.

CLAUDIO
Thus can the demigod Authority
Make us pay down for our offence by weight 120

61

The words of heaven. On whom it will, it will;
On whom it will not, so: yet still 'tis just.

LUCIO

Why, how now, Claudio? Whence comes this restraint?

CLAUDIO

From too much liberty, my Lucio, liberty.
As surfeit is the father of much fast,
So every scope by the immoderate use
Turns to restraint. Our natures do pursue,
Like rats that ravin down their proper bane,
A thirsty evil, and when we drink we die.

130 LUCIO If I could speak so wisely under an arrest, I would
send for certain of my creditors. And yet, to say the
truth, I had as lief have the foppery of freedom as
the mortality of imprisonment. What's thy offence,
Claudio?

CLAUDIO What but to speak of would offend again.

LUCIO What, is't murder?

CLAUDIO No.

LUCIO Lechery?

CLAUDIO Call it so.

140 PROVOST Away, sir, you must go.

CLAUDIO One word, good friend. Lucio, a word with you.

LUCIO

A hundred, if they'll do you any good.
Is lechery so looked after?

CLAUDIO

Thus stands it with me: upon a true contract
I got possession of Julietta's bed.
You know the lady. She is fast my wife
Save that we do denunciation lack
Of outward order. This we came not to,
Only for propagation of a dower
150　Remaining in the coffer of her friends,

From whom we thought it meet to hide our love
Till time had made them for us. But it chances
The stealth of our most mutual entertainment
With character too gross is writ on Juliet.

LUCIO
With child, perhaps?

CLAUDIO   Unhappily, even so.
And the new deputy now for the Duke –
Whether it be the fault and glimpse of newness,
Or whether that the body public be
A horse whereon the governor doth ride,
Who, newly in the seat, that it may know   160
He can command, lets it straight feel the spur;
Whether the tyranny be in his place,
Or in his eminence that fills it up,
I stagger in – but this new governor
Awakes me all the enrollèd penalties
Which have, like unscoured armour, hung by th'wall
So long that nineteen zodiacs have gone round
And none of them been worn, and for a name
Now puts the drowsy and neglected act
Freshly on me. 'Tis surely for a name.   170

LUCIO I warrant it is, an thy head stands so tickle on thy
shoulders that a milkmaid, if she be in love, may sigh it
off. Send after the Duke and appeal to him.

CLAUDIO
I have done so, but he's not to be found.
I prithee, Lucio, do me this kind service:
This day my sister should the cloister enter,
And there receive her approbation.
Acquaint her with the danger of my state,
Implore her, in my voice, that she make friends
To the strict deputy, bid herself assay him.   180
I have great hope in that, for in her youth

There is a prone and speechless dialect,
Such as move men; beside, she hath prosperous art
When she will play with reason and discourse,
And well she can persuade.

LUCIO I pray she may, as well for the encouragement of the
like, which else would stand under grievous imposition,
as for the enjoying of thy life, who I would be sorry
should be thus foolishly lost at a game of tick-tack.
190 I'll to her.

CLAUDIO
I thank you, good friend Lucio.

LUCIO
Within two hours.

CLAUDIO   Come, officer, away.   *Exeunt*

I.3   *Enter Duke and Friar Thomas*

DUKE
No, holy father, throw away that thought;
Believe not that the dribbling dart of love
Can pierce a complete bosom. Why I desire thee
To give me secret harbour hath a purpose
More grave and wrinkled than the aims and ends
Of burning youth.

FRIAR THOMAS   May your grace speak of it?

DUKE
My holy sir, none better knows than you
How I have ever loved the life removed
And held in idle price to haunt assemblies
10 Where youth and cost a witless bravery keeps.
I have delivered to Lord Angelo,
A man of stricture and firm abstinence,
My absolute power and place here in Vienna,
And he supposes me travelled to Poland,

64

For so I have strewed it in the common ear,
And so it is received. Now, pious sir,
You will demand of me why I do this.

FRIAR THOMAS
Gladly, my lord.

DUKE
We have strict statutes and most biting laws,
The needful bits and curbs to headstrong weeds,   20
Which for this fourteen years we have let slip;
Even like an o'ergrown lion in a cave,
That goes not out to prey. Now, as fond fathers,
Having bound up the threatening twigs of birch,
Only to stick it in their children's sight
For terror, not to use, in time the rod
Becomes more mocked than feared, so our decrees,
Dead to infliction, to themselves are dead,
And liberty plucks justice by the nose;
The baby beats the nurse, and quite athwart   30
Goes all decorum.

FRIAR THOMAS   It rested in your grace
To unloose this tied-up justice when you pleased,
And it in you more dreadful would have seemed
Than in Lord Angelo.

DUKE   I do fear, too dreadful.
Sith 'twas my fault to give the people scope,
'Twould be my tyranny to strike and gall them
For what I bid them do: for we bid this be done
When evil deeds have their permissive pass
And not the punishment. Therefore, indeed, my father,
I have on Angelo imposed the office,   40
Who may, in th'ambush of my name, strike home,
And yet my nature never in the sight
To do it slander. And to behold his sway
I will, as 'twere a brother of your order,

Visit both prince and people. Therefore, I prithee,
Supply me with the habit, and instruct
How I may formally in person bear me
Like a true friar. More reasons for this action
At our more leisure shall I render you;
50   Only this one – Lord Angelo is precise,
Stands at a guard with envy, scarce confesses
That his blood flows, or that his appetite
Is more to bread than stone. Hence shall we see,
If power change purpose, what our seemers be. *Exeunt*

I.4   *Enter Isabella and Francisca, a nun*

ISABELLA
And have you nuns no farther privileges?

FRANCISCA
Are not these large enough?

ISABELLA
Yes, truly. I speak not as desiring more,
But rather wishing a more strict restraint
Upon the sisterhood, the votarists of Saint Clare.
    Lucio within

LUCIO
Ho! Peace be in this place.

ISABELLA   Who's that which calls?

FRANCISCA
It is a man's voice. Gentle Isabella,
Turn you the key, and know his business of him.
You may, I may not; you are yet unsworn.
10   When you have vowed, you must not speak with men
But in the presence of the prioress;
Then, if you speak, you must not show your face,
Or, if you show your face, you must not speak.

He calls again. I pray you, answer him.   *Exit*

ISABELLA

Peace and prosperity! Who is't that calls?
  Enter Lucio

LUCIO

Hail, virgin, if you be, as those cheek-roses
Proclaim you are no less. Can you so stead me
As bring me to the sight of Isabella,
A novice of this place, and the fair sister
To her unhappy brother, Claudio?   20

ISABELLA

Why 'her unhappy brother'? Let me ask,
The rather for I now must make you know
I am that Isabella, and his sister.

LUCIO

Gentle and fair, your brother kindly greets you.
Not to be weary with you, he's in prison.

ISABELLA

Woe me, for what?

LUCIO

For that which, if myself might be his judge,
He should receive his punishment in thanks.
He hath got his friend with child.

ISABELLA

Sir, make me not your story.

LUCIO   It is true.   30
I would not, though 'tis my familiar sin
With maids to seem the lapwing and to jest,
Tongue far from heart, play with all virgins so.
I hold you as a thing enskied and sainted,
By your renouncement an immortal spirit
And to be talked with in sincerity,
As with a saint.

ISABELLA

You do blaspheme the good in mocking me.

LUCIO

Do not believe it. Fewness and truth, 'tis thus:
40 Your brother and his lover have embraced.
As those that feed grow full, as blossoming time
That from the seedness the bare fallow brings
To teeming foison, even so her plenteous womb
Expresseth his full tilth and husbandry.

ISABELLA

Someone with child by him? My cousin Juliet?

LUCIO

Is she your cousin?

ISABELLA

Adoptedly, as school-maids change their names
By vain though apt affection.

LUCIO   She it is.

ISABELLA O, let him marry her.

LUCIO   This is the point.
50 The Duke is very strangely gone from hence,
Bore many gentlemen, myself being one,
In hand and hope of action; but we do learn
By those that know the very nerves of state,
His givings-out were of an infinite distance
From his true-meant design. Upon his place,
And with full line of his authority,
Governs Lord Angelo, a man whose blood
Is very snow-broth, one who never feels
The wanton stings and motions of the sense,
60 But doth rebate and blunt his natural edge
With profits of the mind, study, and fast.
He, to give fear to use and liberty,
Which have for long run by the hideous law,
As mice by lions, hath picked out an act,

Under whose heavy sense your brother's life
Falls into forfeit; he arrests him on it,
And follows close the rigour of the statute
To make him an example. All hope is gone,
Unless you have the grace by your fair prayer
To soften Angelo. And that's my pith of business   70
'Twixt you and your poor brother.

ISABELLA

Doth he so seek his life?

LUCIO   Has censured him
Already and, as I hear, the provost hath
A warrant for his execution.

ISABELLA

Alas, what poor ability's in me
To do him good.

LUCIO   Assay the power you have.

ISABELLA

My power? Alas, I doubt.

LUCIO   Our doubts are traitors
And make us lose the good we oft might win,
By fearing to attempt. Go to Lord Angelo,
And let him learn to know, when maidens sue,   80
Men give like gods; but when they weep and kneel,
All their petitions are as freely theirs
As they themselves would owe them.

ISABELLA

I'll see what I can do.

LUCIO   But speedily.

ISABELLA

I will about it straight,
No longer staying but to give the Mother
Notice of my affair. I humbly thank you.
Commend me to my brother. Soon at night
I'll send him certain word of my success.

LUCIO
90   I take my leave of you.

ISABELLA   Good sir, adieu.   *Exeunt*

✳

II.1   *Enter Angelo, Escalus, and Servants, Justice*

ANGELO
    We must not make a scarecrow of the law,
    Setting it up to fear the birds of prey,
    And let it keep one shape, till custom make it
    Their perch and not their terror.

ESCALUS   Ay, but yet
    Let us be keen and rather cut a little
    Than fall, and bruise to death. Alas, this gentleman,
    Whom I would save, had a most noble father.
    Let but your honour know,
    Whom I believe to be most strait in virtue,
10   That, in the working of your own affections,
    Had time cohered with place or place with wishing,
    Or that the resolute acting of your blood
    Could have attained th'effect of your own purpose,
    Whether you had not sometime in your life
    Erred in this point which now you censure him,
    And pulled the law upon you.

ANGELO
    'Tis one thing to be tempted, Escalus,
    Another thing to fall. I not deny,
    The jury, passing on the prisoner's life,
20   May in the sworn twelve have a thief or two
    Guiltier than him they try; what's open made to justice,
    That justice seizes; what knows the laws
    That thieves do pass on thieves? 'Tis very pregnant,

The jewel that we find, we stoop and take't
Because we see it; but what we do not see
We tread upon, and never think of it.
You may not so extenuate his offence
For I have had such faults; but rather tell me,
When I, that censure him, do so offend,
Let mine own judgement pattern out my death   30
And nothing come in partial. Sir, he must die.

Enter Provost

ESCALUS
Be it as your wisdom will.

ANGELO   Where is the provost?

PROVOST
Here, if it like your honour.

ANGELO   See that Claudio
Be executed by tomorrow morning:
Bring his confessor, let him be prepared;
For that's the utmost of his pilgrimage.   *Exit Provost*

ESCALUS
Well, heaven forgive him, and forgive us all.
Some rise by sin, and some by virtue fall:
Some run from brakes of office, and answer none,
And some condemnèd for a fault alone.   40

Enter Elbow, Froth, Pompey, Officers

ELBOW Come, bring them away. If these be good people
in a commonweal that do nothing but use their abuses
in common houses, I know no law. Bring them away.

ANGELO How now, sir, what's your name? And what's
the matter?

ELBOW If it please your honour, I am the poor Duke's
constable, and my name is Elbow. I do lean upon
justice, sir, and do bring in here before your good
honour two notorious benefactors.

ANGELO Benefactors? Well, what benefactors are they? 50

71

Are they not malefactors?

ELBOW If it please your honour, I know not well what they are; but precise villains they are, that I am sure of, and void of all profanation in the world that good Christians ought to have.

ESCALUS This comes off well. Here's a wise officer.

ANGELO Go to. What quality are they of? Elbow is your name? Why dost thou not speak, Elbow?

POMPEY He cannot, sir. He's out at elbow.

60 ANGELO What are you, sir?

ELBOW He, sir? A tapster, sir, parcel-bawd; one that serves a bad woman, whose house, sir, was, as they say, plucked down in the suburbs, and now she professes a hot-house, which I think is a very ill house too.

ESCALUS How know you that?

ELBOW My wife, sir, whom I detest before heaven and your honour –

ESCALUS How? Thy wife?

ELBOW Ay, sir, whom I thank heaven is an honest
70 woman –

ESCALUS Dost thou detest her therefore?

ELBOW I say, sir, I will detest myself also, as well as she, that this house, if it be not a bawd's house, it is pity of her life, for it is a naughty house.

ESCALUS How dost thou know that, constable?

ELBOW Marry, sir, by my wife, who, if she had been a woman cardinally given, might have been accused in fornication, adultery, and all uncleanliness there.

ESCALUS By the woman's means?

80 ELBOW Ay, sir, by Mistress Overdone's means; but as she spit in his face, so she defied him.

POMPEY Sir, if it please your honour, this is not so.

ELBOW Prove it before these varlets here, thou honourable man, prove it.

ESCALUS Do you hear how he misplaces?

POMPEY Sir, she came in great with child, and longing –
saving your honour's reverence – for stewed prunes.
Sir, we had but two in the house, which at that very
distant time stood, as it were, in a fruit dish, a dish of
some threepence; your honours have seen such dishes; 90
they are not china dishes, but very good dishes.

ESCALUS Go to, go to; no matter for the dish, sir.

POMPEY No, indeed, sir, not of a pin; you are therein in
the right: but to the point. As I say, this Mistress
Elbow, being, as I say, with child, and being great-
bellied, and longing, as I said, for prunes, and having
but two in the dish, as I said, Master Froth here, this
very man, having eaten the rest, as I said, and, as I
say, paying for them very honestly, for, as you know,
Master Froth, I could not give you threepence again. 100

FROTH No, indeed.

POMPEY Very well: you being then, if you be remem-
bered, cracking the stones of the foresaid prunes –

FROTH Ay, so I did, indeed.

POMPEY Why, very well: I telling you then, if you be re-
membered, that such a one and such a one were past
cure of the thing you wot of, unless they kept very good
diet, as I told you –

FROTH All this is true.

POMPEY Why, very well then – 110

ESCALUS Come, you are a tedious fool. To the purpose.
What was done to Elbow's wife, that he hath cause to
complain of? Come me to what was done to her.

POMPEY Sir, your honour cannot come to that yet.

ESCALUS No, sir, nor I mean it not.

POMPEY Sir, but you shall come to it, by your honour's
leave. And I beseech you look into Master Froth here,
sir; a man of fourscore pound a year, whose father died

at Hallowmas. Was't not at Hallowmas, Master Froth?

120 FROTH Allhallond Eve.

POMPEY Why, very well. I hope here be truths. He, sir, sitting, as I say, in a lower chair, sir – 'twas in the Bunch of Grapes, where indeed you have a delight to sit, have you not?

FROTH I have so, because it is an open room and good for winter.

POMPEY Why, very well then. I hope here be truths.

ANGELO
This will last out a night in Russia
When nights are longest there. I'll take my leave,
130 And leave you to the hearing of the cause,
Hoping you'll find good cause to whip them all.

ESCALUS I think no less. Good morrow to your lordship.

Exit Angelo

Now, sir, come on. What was done to Elbow's wife, once more?

POMPEY Once, sir? There was nothing done to her once.

ELBOW I beseech you, sir, ask him what this man did to my wife.

POMPEY I beseech your honour, ask me.

ESCALUS Well, sir, what did this gentleman to her?

140 POMPEY I beseech you, sir, look in this gentleman's face. Good Master Froth, look upon his honour; 'tis for a good purpose. Doth your honour mark his face?

ESCALUS Ay, sir, very well.

POMPEY Nay, I beseech you, mark it well.

ESCALUS Well, I do so.

POMPEY Doth your honour see any harm in his face?

ESCALUS Why, no.

POMPEY I'll be supposed upon a book, his face is the worst thing about him. Good then; if his face be the
150 worst thing about him, how could Master Froth do the

constable's wife any harm? I would know that of your
honour.

ESCALUS He's in the right. Constable, what say you to it?

ELBOW First, an it like you, the house is a respected
house; next, this is a respected fellow, and his mistress
is a respected woman.

POMPEY By this hand, sir, his wife is a more respected
person than any of us all.

ELBOW Varlet, thou liest; thou liest, wicked varlet. The
time is yet to come that she was ever respected with man, 160
woman, or child.

POMPEY Sir, she was respected with him before he
married with her.

ESCALUS Which is the wiser here, Justice or Iniquity? Is
this true?

ELBOW O thou caitiff, O thou varlet, O thou wicked
Hannibal! I respected with her before I was married
to her? If ever I was respected with her, or she with
me, let not your worship think me the poor Duke's
officer. Prove this, thou wicked Hannibal, or I'll have 170
mine action of battery on thee.

ESCALUS If he took you a box o'th'ear, you might have
your action of slander, too.

ELBOW Marry, I thank your good worship for it. What
is't your worship's pleasure I shall do with this wicked
caitiff?

ESCALUS Truly, officer, because he hath some offences in
him that thou wouldst discover, if thou couldst, let him
continue in his courses till thou know'st what they are.

ELBOW Marry, I thank your worship for it. Thou seest, 180
thou wicked varlet, now, what's come upon thee. Thou
art to continue now, thou varlet, thou art to continue.

ESCALUS Where were you born, friend?

FROTH Here in Vienna, sir.

ESCALUS Are you of fourscore pounds a year?

FROTH Yes, an't please you, sir.

ESCALUS So. What trade are you of, sir?

POMPEY A tapster, a poor widow's tapster.

ESCALUS Your mistress' name?

190 POMPEY Mistress Overdone.

ESCALUS Hath she had any more than one husband?

POMPEY Nine, sir. Overdone by the last.

ESCALUS Nine? Come hither to me, Master Froth.
Master Froth, I would not have you acquainted with
tapsters; they will draw you, Master Froth, and you will
hang then. Get you gone, and let me hear no more of
you.

FROTH I thank your worship. For mine own part, I
never come into any room in a taphouse but I am drawn
200 in.

ESCALUS Well, no more of it, Master Froth. Farewell.

Exit Froth

Come you hither to me, Master Tapster. What's your
name, Master Tapster?

POMPEY Pompey.

ESCALUS What else?

POMPEY Bum, sir.

ESCALUS Troth, and your bum is the greatest thing about
you, so that, in the beastliest sense, you are Pompey the
Great. Pompey, you are partly a bawd, Pompey, how-
210 soever you colour it in being a tapster, are you not?
Come, tell me true. It shall be the better for you.

POMPEY Truly, sir, I am a poor fellow that would live.

ESCALUS How would you live, Pompey? By being a
bawd? What do you think of the trade, Pompey? Is it a
lawful trade?

POMPEY If the law would allow it, sir.

ESCALUS But the law will not allow it, Pompey; nor it

shall not be allowed in Vienna.

POMPEY Does your worship mean to geld and splay all
the youth of the city? 220

ESCALUS No, Pompey.

POMPEY Truly, sir, in my poor opinion, they will to't
then. If your worship will take order for the drabs and
the knaves, you need not to fear the bawds.

ESCALUS There is pretty orders beginning, I can tell you.
It is but heading and hanging.

POMPEY If you head and hang all that offend that way
but for ten year together, you'll be glad to give out a
commission for more heads. If this law hold in Vienna
ten year, I'll rent the fairest house in it after threepence 230
a bay. If you live to see this come to pass, say Pompey
told you so.

ESCALUS Thank you, good Pompey, and, in requital of
your prophecy, hark you: I advise you, let me not find
you before me again upon any complaint whatsoever;
no, not for dwelling where you do. If I do, Pompey, I
shall beat you to your tent, and prove a shrewd Caesar
to you. In plain dealing, Pompey, I shall have you
whipped. So, for this time, Pompey, fare you well.

POMPEY I thank your worship for your good counsel; 240
but I shall follow it as the flesh and fortune shall better
determine.
Whip me? No, no, let carman whip his jade.
The valiant heart's not whipped out of his trade. *Exit*

ESCALUS Come hither to me, Master Elbow. Come
hither, master constable. How long have you been in
this place of constable?

ELBOW Seven year and a half, sir.

ESCALUS I thought, by your readiness in the office, you
had continued in it some time. You say, seven years to- 250
gether?

ELBOW And a half, sir.

ESCALUS Alas, it hath been great pains to you; they do
you wrong to put you so oft upon't. Are there not men in
your ward sufficient to serve it?

ELBOW Faith, sir, few of any wit in such matters. As they
are chosen, they are glad to choose me for them. I do it
for some piece of money, and go through with all.

ESCALUS Look you bring me in the names of some six or
260   seven, the most sufficient of your parish.

ELBOW To your worship's house, sir?

ESCALUS To my house. Fare you well.   *Exit Elbow*
What's o'clock, think you?

JUSTICE Eleven, sir.

ESCALUS I pray you home to dinner with me.

JUSTICE I humbly thank you.

ESCALUS

  It grieves me for the death of Claudio,
  But there's no remedy.

JUSTICE

  Lord Angelo is severe.

ESCALUS   It is but needful.
270   Mercy is not itself, that oft looks so;
  Pardon is still the nurse of second woe.
  But yet poor Claudio; there is no remedy.
  Come, sir.   *Exeunt*

II.2   *Enter Provost, and a Servant*

SERVANT

  He's hearing of a cause; he will come straight;
  I'll tell him of you.

PROVOST   Pray you, do. *Exit Servant*
                          I'll know
  His pleasure; maybe he'll relent. Alas,
  He hath but as offended in a dream.

All sects, all ages smack of this vice, and he
To die for it!

    Enter Angelo

ANGELO   Now, what's the matter, provost?

PROVOST

Is it your will Claudio shall die tomorrow?

ANGELO

Did not I tell thee, yea? Hadst thou not order?
Why dost thou ask again?

PROVOST   Lest I might be too rash.
Under your good correction, I have seen   10
When, after execution, judgement hath
Repented o'er his doom.

ANGELO   Go to; let that be mine.
Do you your office, or give up your place,
And you shall well be spared.

PROVOST   I crave your honour's pardon.
What shall be done, sir, with the groaning Juliet?
She's very near her hour.

ANGELO   Dispose of her
To some more fitter place, and that with speed.

    Enter Servant

SERVANT

Here is the sister of the man condemned
Desires access to you.

ANGELO   Hath he a sister?

PROVOST

Ay, my good lord, a very virtuous maid,   20
And to be shortly of a sisterhood,
If not already.

ANGELO   Well, let her be admitted.   *Exit Servant*
See you the fornicatress be removed;
Let her have needful, but not lavish, means.
There shall be order for't.

Enter Lucio and Isabella

PROVOST   God save your nonour.

ANGELO

    Stay a little while. (*To Isabella*) Y'are welcome. What's
        your will?

ISABELLA

    I am a woeful suitor to your honour,
    Please but your honour hear me.

ANGELO   Well, what's your suit?

ISABELLA

    There is a vice that most I do abhor,
30   And most desire should meet the blow of justice,
    For which I would not plead, but that I must,
    For which I must not plead, but that I am
    At war 'twixt will and will not.

ANGELO   Well: the matter?

ISABELLA

    I have a brother is condemned to die.
    I do beseech you, let it be his fault,
    And not my brother.

PROVOST (*aside*)   Heaven give thee moving graces.

ANGELO

    Condemn the fault, and not the actor of it?
    Why, every fault's condemned ere it be done.
    Mine were the very cipher of a function,
40   To fine the faults whose fine stands in record,
    And let go by the actor.

ISABELLA   O just, but severe law!
    I had a brother then; heaven keep your honour.

LUCIO (*aside to Isabella*)

    Give't not o'er so. To him again, entreat him,
    Kneel down before him, hang upon his gown;
    You are too cold. If you should need a pin,
    You could not with more tame a tongue desire it.

To him, I say.

ISABELLA
Must he needs die?

ANGELO   Maiden, no remedy.

ISABELLA
Yes, I do think that you might pardon him,
And neither heaven nor man grieve at the mercy.   50

ANGELO
I will not do't.

ISABELLA   But can you if you would?

ANGELO
Look what I will not, that I cannot do.

ISABELLA
But might you do't, and do the world no wrong,
If so your heart were touched with that remorse
As mine is to him?

ANGELO
He's sentenced; 'tis too late.

LUCIO (*aside to Isabella*)   You are too cold.

ISABELLA
Too late? Why, no. I that do speak a word
May call it back again. Well, believe this,
No ceremony that to great ones longs,
Not the king's crown, nor the deputed sword,   60
The marshal's truncheon, nor the judge's robe,
Become them with one half so good a grace
As mercy does.
If he had been as you, and you as he,
You would have slipped like him; but he, like you,
Would not have been so stern.

ANGELO   Pray you, be gone.

ISABELLA
I would to heaven I had your potency,
And you were Isabel; should it then be thus?

No, I would tell what 'twere to be a judge,
70 And what a prisoner.

LUCIO *(aside to Isabella)*

Ay, touch him; there's the vein.

ANGELO

Your brother is a forfeit of the law,
And you but waste your words.

ISABELLA   Alas, alas;

Why, all the souls that were were forfeit once,
And He that might the vantage best have took
Found out the remedy. How would you be,
If He, which is the top of judgement, should
But judge you as you are? O think on that,
And mercy then will breathe within your lips,
Like man new made.

ANGELO   Be you content, fair maid,
80 It is the law, not I, condemns your brother;
Were he my kinsman, brother, or my son,
It should be thus with him. He must die tomorrow.

ISABELLA

Tomorrow? O, that's sudden; spare him, spare him.
He's not prepared for death. Even for our kitchens
We kill the fowl of season. Shall we serve heaven
With less respect than we do minister
To our gross selves? Good, good my lord, bethink you:
Who is it that hath died for this offence?
There's many have committed it.

LUCIO *(aside to Isabella)*   Ay, well said.

ANGELO

90 The law hath not been dead, though it hath slept.
Those many had not dared to do that evil
If that the first that did th'edict infringe
Had answered for his deed. Now 'tis awake,
Takes note of what is done, and like a prophet

Looks in a glass that shows what future evils,
Either now, or by remissness new, conceived,
And so in progress to be hatched and born,
Are now to have no successive degrees,
But, ere they live, to end.

ISABELLA   Yet show some pity.

ANGELO

I show it most of all when I show justice,   100
For then I pity those I do not know,
Which a dismissed offence would after gall,
And do him right that, answering one foul wrong,
Lives not to act another. Be satisfied
Your brother dies tomorrow. Be content.

ISABELLA

So you must be the first that gives this sentence,
And he, that suffers. O, 'tis excellent
To have a giant's strength, but it is tyrannous
To use it like a giant.

LUCIO (*aside to Isabella*) That's well said.

ISABELLA

Could great men thunder   110
As Jove himself does, Jove would ne'er be quiet,
For every pelting, petty officer
Would use his heaven for thunder,
Nothing but thunder. Merciful heaven,
Thou rather with thy sharp and sulphurous bolt
Splits the unwedgeable and gnarlèd oak
Than the soft myrtle; but man, proud man,
Dressed in a little brief authority,
Most ignorant of what he's most assured,
His glassy essence, like an angry ape   120
Plays such fantastic tricks before high heaven
As makes the angels weep; who, with our spleens,
Would all themselves laugh mortal.

LUCIO (*aside to Isabella*)

O, to him, to him, wench; he will relent.

He's coming, I perceive't.

PROVOST (*aside*)   Pray heaven she win him.

ISABELLA

We cannot weigh our brother with ourself.

Great men may jest with saints: 'tis wit in them,

But in the less, foul profanation.

LUCIO (*aside to Isabella*)

Thou'rt i'th'right, girl, more o'that.

ISABELLA

130 That in the captain's but a choleric word

Which in the soldier is flat blasphemy.

LUCIO (*aside to Isabella*)

Art avised o'that? More on't.

ANGELO

Why do you put these sayings upon me?

ISABELLA

Because authority, though it err like others,

Hath yet a kind of medicine in itself

That skins the vice o'th'top. Go to your bosom,

Knock there, and ask your heart what it doth know

That's like my brother's fault; if it confess

A natural guiltiness such as is his,

140 Let it not sound a thought upon your tongue

Against my brother's life.

ANGELO (*aside*)   She speaks, and 'tis

Such sense that my sense breeds with it. Fare you well.

ISABELLA

Gentle my lord, turn back.

ANGELO

I will bethink me. Come again tomorrow.

ISABELLA

Hark how I'll bribe you. Good my lord, turn back.

ANGELO
How? Bribe me?

ISABELLA
Ay, with such gifts that heaven shall share with you.

LUCIO (*aside to Isabella*)
You had marred all else.

ISABELLA
Not with fond sicles of the tested gold,
Or stones whose rate are either rich or poor   150
As fancy values them; but with true prayers
That shall be up at heaven and enter there
Ere sunrise: prayers from preservèd souls,
From fasting maids whose minds are dedicate
To nothing temporal.

ANGELO   Well, come to me tomorrow.

LUCIO (*aside to Isabella*)
Go to, 'tis well; away.

ISABELLA
Heaven keep your honour safe.

ANGELO (*aside*)   Amen.
For I am that way going to temptation,
Where prayers cross.

ISABELLA   At what hour tomorrow
Shall I attend your lordship?

ANGELO   At any time 'forenoon.   160

ISABELLA
God save your honour.
                    Exeunt Isabella, Lucio, and Provost

ANGELO   From thee: even from thy virtue.
What's this? What's this? Is this her fault or mine?
The tempter, or the tempted, who sins most?
Ha?
Not she, nor doth she tempt; but it is I
That, lying by the violet in the sun,

Do as the carrion does, not as the flower,
Corrupt with virtuous season. Can it be
That modesty may more betray our sense
170 Than woman's lightness? Having waste ground enough,
Shall we desire to raze the sanctuary
And pitch our evils there? O fie, fie, fie!
What dost thou? Or what art thou, Angelo?
Dost thou desire her foully for those things
That make her good? O, let her brother live:
Thieves for their robbery have authority
When judges steal themselves. What, do I love her,
That I desire to hear her speak again,
And feast upon her eyes? What is't I dream on?
180 O cunning enemy that, to catch a saint,
With saints dost bait thy hook. Most dangerous
Is that temptation that doth goad us on
To sin in loving virtue. Never could the strumpet
With all her double vigour, art and nature,
Once stir my temper; but this virtuous maid
Subdues me quite. Ever till now,
When men were fond, I smiled and wondered how.

Exit

II.3   *Enter Duke, disguised as a friar, and Provost*
DUKE

Hail to you, provost – so I think you are.
PROVOST

I am the provost. What's your will, good friar?
DUKE

Bound by my charity and my blessed order,
I come to visit the afflicted spirits
Here in the prison. Do me the common right
To let me see them and to make me know
The nature of their crimes, that I may minister

To them accordingly.

PROVOST

I would do more than that, if more were needful.

Enter Juliet

Look, here comes one: a gentlewoman of mine,   10
Who, falling in the flaws of her own youth,
Hath blistered her report. She is with child,
And he that got it, sentenced: a young man
More fit to do another such offence
Than die for this.

DUKE

When must he die?

PROVOST   As I do think, tomorrow.

(*To Juliet*) I have provided for you; stay a while
And you shall be conducted.

DUKE

Repent you, fair one, of the sin you carry?

JULIET

I do, and bear the shame most patiently.   20

DUKE

I'll teach you how you shall arraign your conscience
And try your penitence, if it be sound,
Or hollowly put on.

JULIET   I'll gladly learn.

DUKE

Love you the man that wronged you?

JULIET

Yes, as I love the woman that wronged him.

DUKE

So then it seems your most offenceful act
Was mutually committed?

JULIET   Mutually.

DUKE

Then was your sin of heavier kind than his.

JULIET
  I do confess it, and repent it, father.

DUKE
30 'Tis meet so, daughter, but lest you do repent
  As that the sin hath brought you to this shame,
  Which sorrow is always toward ourselves, not heaven,
  Showing we would not spare heaven as we love it,
  But as we stand in fear –

JULIET
  I do repent me as it is an evil,
  And take the shame with joy.

DUKE   There rest.
  Your partner, as I hear, must die tomorrow,
  And I am going with instruction to him.
  Grace go with you. *Benedicite*.   *Exit*

JULIET
40 Must die tomorrow? O injurious love,
  That respites me a life whose very comfort
  Is still a dying horror.

PROVOST   'Tis pity of him.   *Exeunt*

II.4   *Enter Angelo*

ANGELO
  When I would pray and think, I think and pray
  To several subjects: heaven hath my empty words,
  Whilst my invention, hearing not my tongue,
  Anchors on Isabel: God in my mouth,
  As if I did but only chew His name,
  And in my heart the strong and swelling evil
  Of my conception. The state, whereon I studied,
  Is like a good thing, being often read,
  Grown seared and tedious; yea, my gravity,
10 Wherein, let no man hear me, I take pride,

Could I, with boot, change for an idle plume
Which the air beats for vain. O place, O form,
How often dost thou with thy case, thy habit,
Wrench awe from fools, and tie the wiser souls
To thy false seeming! Blood, thou art blood;
Let's write 'good Angel' on the devil's horn,
'Tis not the devil's crest – How now? Who's there?

Enter Servant

SERVANT

One Isabel, a sister, desires access to you.

ANGELO

Teach her the way.   *Exit Servant*
              O heavens,
Why does my blood thus muster to my heart,   20
Making both it unable for itself,
And dispossessing all my other parts
Of necessary fitness?
So play the foolish throngs with one that swoons,
Come all to help him, and so stop the air
By which he should revive; and even so
The general, subject to a well-wished king,
Quit their own part, and in obsequious fondness
Crowd to his presence, where their untaught love
Must needs appear offence.

Enter Isabella

                          How now, fair maid!   30

ISABELLA

I am come to know your pleasure.

ANGELO

That you might know it, would much better please me
Than to demand what 'tis. Your brother cannot live.

ISABELLA

Even so. Heaven keep your honour.

ANGELO

Yet may he live a while; and it may be
As long as you or I, yet he must die.

ISABELLA

Under your sentence?

ANGELO

Yea.

ISABELLA

When, I beseech you? That in his reprieve,
40   Longer or shorter, he may be so fitted
That his soul sicken not.

ANGELO

Ha! fie, these filthy vices! It were as good
To pardon him that hath from nature stol'n
A man already made as to remit
Their saucy sweetness that do coin God's image
In stamps that are forbid: 'tis all as easy
Falsely to take away a life true made
As to put metal in restrainèd means
To make a false one.

ISABELLA

50   'Tis set down so in heaven, but not in earth.

ANGELO

Say you so? Then I shall pose you quickly.
Which had you rather, that the most just law
Now took your brother's life, or to redeem him
Give up your body to such sweet uncleanness
As she that he hath stained?

ISABELLA   Sir, believe this,
I had rather give my body than my soul.

ANGELO

I talk not of your soul. Our compelled sins
Stand more for number than accompt.

ISABELLA   How say you?

ANGELO

   Nay, I'll not warrant that, for I can speak
   Against the thing I say. Answer to this: 60
   I, now the voice of the recorded law,
   Pronounce a sentence on your brother's life;
   Might there not be a charity in sin
   To save this brother's life?

ISABELLA   Please you to do't,
   I'll take it as a peril to my soul;
   It is no sin at all, but charity.

ANGELO

   Pleased you to do't, at peril of your soul,
   Were equal poise of sin and charity.

ISABELLA

   That I do beg his life, if it be sin,
   Heaven let me bear it: you granting of my suit,   70
   If that be sin, I'll make it my morn prayer
   To have it added to the faults of mine
   And nothing of your answer.

ANGELO   Nay, but hear me;
   Your sense pursues not mine. Either you are ignorant,
   Or seem so craftily; and that's not good.

ISABELLA

   Let me be ignorant, and in nothing good
   But graciously to know I am no better.

ANGELO

   Thus wisdom wishes to appear most bright
   When it doth tax itself, as these black masks
   Proclaim an enshield beauty ten times louder   80
   Than beauty could, displayed. But mark me;
   To be receivèd plain, I'll speak more gross:
   Your brother is to die.

ISABELLA

   So.

ANGELO

  And his offence is so, as it appears,
  Accountant to the law upon that pain.

ISABELLA

  True.

ANGELO

  Admit no other way to save his life –
  As I subscribe not that, nor any other,
90 But in the loss of question – that you, his sister,
  Finding yourself desired of such a person
  Whose credit with the judge, or own great place,
  Could fetch your brother from the manacles
  Of the all-binding law; and that there were
  No earthly mean to save him, but that either
  You must lay down the treasures of your body
  To this supposed, or else to let him suffer,
  What would you do?

ISABELLA

  As much for my poor brother as myself:
100 That is, were I under the terms of death,
  Th'impression of keen whips I'd wear as rubies,
  And strip myself to death as to a bed
  That long I have been sick for, ere I'd yield
  My body up to shame.

ANGELO   Then must your brother die.

ISABELLA

  And 'twere the cheaper way.
  Better it were a brother died at once
  Than that a sister, by redeeming him,
  Should die for ever.

ANGELO

  Were not you then as cruel as the sentence
110 That you have slandered so?

ISABELLA

    Ignomy in ransom and free pardon
    Are of two houses: lawful mercy is
    Nothing kin to foul redemption.

ANGELO

    You seemed of late to make the law a tyrant,
    And rather proved the sliding of your brother
    A merriment than a vice.

ISABELLA

    O pardon me, my lord; it oft falls out
    To have what we would have, we speak not what we
        mean.
    I something do excuse the thing I hate
    For his advantage that I dearly love.   120

ANGELO

    We are all frail.

ISABELLA   Else let my brother die,
    If not a fedary, but only he
    Owe and succeed thy weakness.

ANGELO

    Nay, women are frail too.

ISABELLA

    Ay, as the glasses where they view themselves,
    Which are as easy broke as they make forms.
    Women, help heaven! Men their creation mar
    In profiting by them. Nay, call us ten times frail,
    For we are soft as our complexions are,
    And credulous to false prints.

ANGELO   I think it well,   130
    And from this testimony of your own sex –
    Since I suppose we are made to be no stronger
    Than faults may shake our frames – let me be bold.
    I do arrest your words. Be that you are,

That is, a woman; if you be more, you're none.
If you be one, as you are well expressed
By all external warrants, show it now,
By putting on the destined livery.

ISABELLA

I have no tongue but one. Gentle my lord,
140 Let me entreat you speak the former language.

ANGELO

Plainly conceive, I love you.

ISABELLA

My brother did love Juliet,
And you tell me that he shall die for't.

ANGELO

He shall not, Isabel, if you give me love.

ISABELLA

I know your virtue hath a licence in't,
Which seems a little fouler than it is,
To pluck on others.

ANGELO   Believe me, on mine honour,
My words express my purpose.

ISABELLA

Ha! Little honour to be much believed,
150 And most pernicious purpose. Seeming, seeming!
I will proclaim thee, Angelo, look for't!
Sign me a present pardon for my brother,
Or with an outstretched throat I'll tell the world
What man thou art.

ANGELO   Who will believe thee, Isabel?
My unsoiled name, th'austereness of my life,
My vouch against you, and my place i'th'state,
Will so your accusation overweigh
That you shall stifle in your own report
And smell of calumny. I have begun,
160 And now I give my sensual race the rein.

Fit thy consent to my sharp appetite,
Lay by all nicety and prolixious blushes,
That banish what they sue for. Redeem thy brother
By yielding up thy body to my will,
Or else he must not only die the death,
But thy unkindness shall his death draw out
To lingering sufferance. Answer me tomorrow,
Or, by the affection that now guides me most,
I'll prove a tyrant to him. As for you,
Say what you can, my false o'erweighs your true. *Exit* 170

ISABELLA

To whom should I complain? Did I tell this,
Who would believe me? O perilous mouths,
That bear in them one and the selfsame tongue,
Either of condemnation or approof,
Bidding the law make curtsy to their will,
Hooking both right and wrong to th'appetite,
To follow as it draws. I'll to my brother.
Though he hath fall'n by prompture of the blood,
Yet hath he in him such a mind of honour
That, had he twenty heads to tender down 180
On twenty bloody blocks, he'd yield them up,
Before his sister should her body stoop
To such abhorred pollution.
Then, Isabel, live chaste, and, brother, die.
More than our brother is our chastity.
I'll tell him yet of Angelo's request,
And fit his mind to death, for his soul's rest. *Exit*

✳

Enter Duke, as a friar, Claudio, and Provost

DUKE

So then you hope of pardon from Lord Angelo?

CLAUDIO

The miserable have no other medicine
But only hope:
I have hope to live, and am prepared to die.

UKE

Be absolute for death: either death or life
Shall thereby be the sweeter. Reason thus with life:
If I do lose thee, I do lose a thing
That none but fools would keep; a breath thou art,
Servile to all the skyey influences

10   That dost this habitation where thou keep'st
Hourly afflict. Merely, thou art death's fool,
For him thou labour'st by thy flight to shun,
And yet runn'st toward him still. Thou art not noble,
For all th'accommodations that thou bear'st
Are nursed by baseness. Thou'rt by no means valiant,
For thou dost fear the soft and tender fork
Of a poor worm. Thy best of rest is sleep,
And that thou oft provok'st, yet grossly fear'st
Thy death, which is no more. Thou art not thyself,

20   For thou exists on many a thousand grains
That issue out of dust. Happy thou art not,
For what thou hast not, still thou striv'st to get,
And what thou hast, forget'st. Thou art not certain,
For thy complexion shifts to strange effects,
After the moon. If thou art rich, thou'rt poor,
For, like an ass, whose back with ingots bows,
Thou bear'st thy heavy riches but a journey,
And death unloads thee. Friend hast thou none,
For thine own bowels, which do call thee sire,

30   The mere effusion of thy proper loins,

Do curse the gout, serpigo, and the rheum
For ending thee no sooner. Thou hast nor youth nor age,
But as it were an after-dinner's sleep,
Dreaming on both, for all thy blessed youth
Becomes as agèd, and doth beg the alms
Of palsied eld: and when thou art old and rich,
Thou hast neither heat, affection, limb, nor beauty
To make thy riches pleasant. What's yet in this
That bears the name of life? Yet in this life
Lie hid more thousand deaths; yet death we fear,   40
That makes these odds all even.

CLAUDIO   I humbly thank you.
To sue to live, I find I seek to die,
And, seeking death, find life. Let it come on.

Enter Isabella

ISABELLA What, ho! Peace here, grace and good company.

PROVOST Who's there? Come in. The wish deserves a
welcome.

DUKE Dear sir, ere long I'll visit you again.

CLAUDIO Most holy sir, I thank you.

ISABELLA My business is a word or two with Claudio.   50

PROVOST And very welcome. Look, signor, here's your
sister.

DUKE Provost, a word with you.

PROVOST As many as you please.

DUKE Bring me to hear them speak, where I may be concealed.

Duke and Provost retire

CLAUDIO Now, sister, what's the comfort?

ISABELLA
Why,
As all comforts are: most good, most good indeed.
Lord Angelo, having affairs to heaven,   60

97

Intends you for his swift ambassador,
Where you shall be an everlasting leiger.
Therefore your best appointment make with speed;
Tomorrow you set on.

CLAUDIO   Is there no remedy?

ISABELLA

None, but such remedy as, to save a head,
To cleave a heart in twain.

CLAUDIO   But is there any?

ISABELLA

Yes, brother, you may live;
There is a devilish mercy in the judge,
If you'll implore it, that will free your life,
70 But fetter you till death.

CLAUDIO   Perpetual durance?

ISABELLA

Ay, just. Perpetual durance, a restraint,
Though all the world's vastidity you had,
To a determined scope.

CLAUDIO   But in what nature?

ISABELLA

In such a one as, you consenting to't,
Would bark your honour from that trunk you bear,
And leave you naked.

CLAUDIO   Let me know the point.

ISABELLA

O, I do fear thee, Claudio, and I quake
Lest thou a feverous life shouldst entertain,
And six or seven winters more respect
80 Than a perpetual honour. Dar'st thou die?
The sense of death is most in apprehension,
And the poor beetle that we tread upon
In corporal sufferance finds a pang as great
As when a giant dies.

CLAUDIO   Why give you me this shame?
　　Think you I can a resolution fetch
　　From flowery tenderness? If I must die,
　　I will encounter darkness as a bride,
　　And hug it in mine arms.

ISABELLA
　　There spake my brother. There my father's grave
　　Did utter forth a voice. Yes, thou must die.   90
　　Thou art too noble to conserve a life
　　In base appliances. This outward-sainted deputy,
　　Whose settled visage and deliberate word
　　Nips youth i'th'head, and follies doth enew
　　As falcon doth the fowl, is yet a devil.
　　His filth within being cast, he would appear
　　A pond as deep as hell.

CLAUDIO   The precise Angelo?

ISABELLA
　　O, 'tis the cunning livery of hell,
　　The damnèd'st body to invest and cover
　　In precious guards. Dost thou think, Claudio,   100
　　If I would yield him my virginity,
　　Thou might'st be freed?

CLAUDIO   O heavens, it cannot be.

ISABELLA
　　Yes, he would give't thee, from this rank offence,
　　So to offend him still. This night's the time
　　That I should do what I abhor to name,
　　Or else thou diest tomorrow.

CLAUDIO   Thou shalt not do't.

ISABELLA
　　O, were it but my life,
　　I'd throw it down for your deliverance
　　As frankly as a pin.

CLAUDIO   Thanks, dear Isabel

ISABELLA

110   Be ready, Claudio, for your death tomorrow.

CLAUDIO

Yes. Has he affections in him
That thus can make him bite the law by th'nose,
When he would force it? Sure it is no sin,
Or of the deadly seven it is the least.

ISABELLA

Which is the least?

CLAUDIO

If it were damnable, he being so wise,
Why would he for the momentary trick
Be perdurably fined? O Isabel!

ISABELLA

What says my brother?

CLAUDIO   Death is a fearful thing.

ISABELLA

120   And shamèd life a hateful.

CLAUDIO

Ay, but to die, and go we know not where,
To lie in cold obstruction and to rot;
This sensible warm motion to become
A kneaded clod; and the delighted spirit
To bathe in fiery floods, or to reside
In thrilling region of thick-ribbèd ice,
To be imprisoned in the viewless winds
And blown with restless violence round about
The pendent world; or to be worse than worst
130   Of those that lawless and incertain thought
Imagine howling, 'tis too horrible.
The weariest and most loathèd worldly life
That age, ache, penury, and imprisonment
Can lay on nature is a paradise
To what we fear of death.

ISABELLA
  Alas, alas.
CLAUDIO Sweet sister, let me live.
  What sin you do to save a brother's life,
  Nature dispenses with the deed so far
  That it becomes a virtue.
ISABELLA   O you beast!
  O faithless coward! O dishonest wretch!   140
  Wilt thou be made a man out of my vice?
  Is't not a kind of incest to take life
  From thine own sister's shame? What should I think?
  Heaven shield my mother played my father fair,
  For such a warpèd slip of wilderness
  Ne'er issued from his blood. Take my defiance,
  Die, perish. Might but my bending down
  Reprieve thee from thy fate, it should proceed.
  I'll pray a thousand prayers for thy death,
  No word to save thee.   150

CLAUDIO
  Nay, hear me, Isabel.
ISABELLA   O, fie, fie, fie!
  Thy sin's not accidental, but a trade.
  Mercy to thee would prove itself a bawd,
  'Tis best that thou diest quickly.   *Going*
CLAUDIO   O hear me, Isabella.
    Duke comes forward
DUKE Vouchsafe a word, young sister, but one word.
ISABELLA What is your will?
DUKE Might you dispense with your leisure, I would by
  and by have some speech with you. The satisfaction I
  would require is likewise your own benefit.
ISABELLA I have no superfluous leisure. My stay must be   160
  stolen out of other affairs, but I will attend you a while.
DUKE (*aside*) Son, I have overheard what hath passed

between you and your sister. Angelo had never the purpose to corrupt her; only he hath made an assay of her virtue to practise his judgement with the disposition of natures. She, having the truth of honour in her, hath made him that gracious denial which he is most glad to receive. I am confessor to Angelo, and I know this to be true. Therefore prepare yourself to death. Do not
170 satisfy your resolution with hopes that are fallible. Tomorrow you must die. Go to your knees and make ready.

CLAUDIO Let me ask my sister pardon. I am so out of love with life that I will sue to be rid of it.

DUKE Hold you there. Farewell. *Exit Claudio*
Enter Provost
Provost, a word with you.

PROVOST What's your will, father?

DUKE That now you are come, you will be gone. Leave me a while with the maid. My mind promises with my
18c habit no loss shall touch her by my company.

PROVOST In good time. *Exit*

DUKE The hand that hath made you fair hath made you good. The goodness that is cheap in beauty makes beauty brief in goodness, but grace, being the soul of your complexion, shall keep the body of it ever fair. The assault that Angelo hath made to you, fortune hath conveyed to my understanding, and, but that frailty hath examples for his falling, I should wonder at Angelo. How will you do to content this substitute,
190 and to save your brother?

ISABELLA I am now going to resolve him. I had rather my brother die by the law than my son should be unlawfully born. But O, how much is the good Duke deceived in Angelo! If ever he return and I can speak to

him, I will open my lips in vain, or discover his government.

DUKE That shall not be much amiss. Yet, as the matter
now stands, he will avoid your accusation; he made trial
of you only. Therefore fasten your ear on my advisings.
To the love I have in doing good a remedy presents 200
itself. I do make myself believe that you may most
uprighteously do a poor wronged lady a merited benefit,
redeem your brother from the angry law, do no stain
to your own gracious person, and much please the
absent Duke, if peradventure he shall ever return to
have hearing of this business.

ISABELLA Let me hear you speak farther. I have spirit to
do anything that appears not foul in the truth of my
spirit.

DUKE Virtue is bold, and goodness never fearful. Have 210
you not heard speak of Mariana, the sister of Frederick,
the great soldier who miscarried at sea?

ISABELLA I have heard of the lady, and good words went
with her name.

DUKE She should this Angelo have married, was affianced
to her by oath, and the nuptial appointed, between
which time of the contract and limit of the solemnity,
her brother Frederick was wrecked at sea, having in that
perished vessel the dowry of his sister. But mark how
heavily this befell to the poor gentlewoman. There she 220
lost a noble and renowned brother, in his love toward
her ever most kind and natural; with him the portion
and sinew of her fortune, her marriage dowry; with
both, her combinate husband, this well-seeming
Angelo.

ISABELLA Can this be so? Did Angelo so leave her?

DUKE Left her in her tears, and dried not one of them

with his comfort, swallowed his vows whole, pretending in her discoveries of dishonour. In few, bestowed her on her own lamentation, which she yet wears for his sake, and he, a marble to her tears, is washed with them, but relents not.

ISABELLA What a merit were it in death to take this poor maid from the world! What corruption in this life, that it will let this man live! But how out of this can she avail?

DUKE It is a rupture that you may easily heal, and the cure of it not only saves your brother, but keeps you from dishonour in doing it.

ISABELLA Show me how, good father.

DUKE This forenamed maid hath yet in her the continuance of her first affection. His unjust unkindness, that in all reason should have quenched her love, hath, like an impediment in the current, made it more violent and unruly. Go you to Angelo, answer his requiring with a plausible obedience, agree with his demands to the point. Only refer yourself to this advantage: first, that your stay with him may not be long, that the time may have all shadow and silence in it, and the place answer to convenience. This being granted in course – and now follows all – we shall advise this wronged maid to stead up your appointment, go in your place. If the encounter acknowledge itself hereafter, it may compel him to her recompense, and here, by this is your brother saved, your honour untainted, the poor Mariana advantaged, and the corrupt deputy scaled. The maid will I frame and make fit for his attempt. If you think well to carry this, as you may, the doubleness of the benefit defends the deceit from reproof. What think you of it?

ISABELLA The image of it gives me content already, and I trust it will grow to a most prosperous perfection.

DUKE It lies much in your holding up. Haste you speedily
to Angelo. If for this night he entreat you to his bed,
give him promise of satisfaction. I will presently to
Saint Luke's. There, at the moated grange, resides this
dejected Mariana. At that place call upon me, and dispatch with Angelo, that it may be quickly.

ISABELLA I thank you for this comfort. Fare you well,
good father. *Exit*

Enter Elbow, Pompey, and Officers III.2

ELBOW Nay, if there be no remedy for it but that you will
needs buy and sell men and women like beasts, we shall
have all the world drink brown and white bastard.

DUKE O heavens, what stuff is here?

POMPEY 'Twas never merry world since, of two usuries,
the merriest was put down, and the worser allowed by
order of law a furred gown to keep him warm; and
furred with fox and lamb skins too, to signify that craft,
being richer than innocency, stands for the facing.

ELBOW Come your way, sir. Bless you, good father friar. 10

DUKE And you, good brother father. What offence hath
this man made you, sir?

ELBOW Marry, sir, he hath offended the law. And, sir, we
take him to be a thief too, sir, for we have found upon
him, sir, a strange picklock, which we have sent to the
deputy.

DUKE
Fie, sirrah, a bawd, a wicked bawd!
The evil that thou causest to be done,
That is thy means to live. Do thou but think
What 'tis to cram a maw or clothe a back 20
From such a filthy vice. Say to thyself,
From their abominable and beastly touches
I drink, I eat, array myself, and live.
Canst thou believe thy living is a life,

So stinkingly depending? Go mend, go mend.

POMPEY Indeed, it does stink in some sort, sir, but yet, sir, I would prove –

DUKE

Nay, if the devil have given thee proofs for sin,
Thou wilt prove his. Take him to prison, officer.
30 Correction and instruction must both work
Ere this rude beast will profit.

ELBOW He must before the deputy, sir. He has given him warning. The deputy cannot abide a whoremaster. If he be a whoremonger, and comes before him, he were as good go a mile on his errand.

DUKE

That we were all, as some would seem to be,
Free from our faults, as faults from seeming free.

Enter Lucio

ELBOW His neck will come to your waist – a cord, sir.

POMPEY I spy comfort, I cry bail. Here's a gentleman and
40 a friend of mine.

LUCIO How now, noble Pompey? What, at the wheels of Caesar? Art thou led in triumph? What, is there none of Pygmalion's images, newly made woman, to be had now, for putting the hand in the pocket and extracting it clutched? What reply? Ha? What say'st thou to this tune, matter, and method? Is't not drowned i'th'last rain, ha? What say'st thou, trot? Is the world as it was, man? Which is the way? Is it sad, and few words? Or how? The trick of it?

50 DUKE Still thus, and thus, still worse?

LUCIO How doth my dear morsel, thy mistress? Procures she still, ha?

POMPEY Troth, sir, she hath eaten up all her beef, and she is herself in the tub.

LUCIO Why, 'tis good. It is the right of it. It must be so.

Ever your fresh whore and your powdered bawd. An
unshunned consequence, it must be so. Art going to
prison, Pompey?

POMPEY Yes, faith, sir.

LUCIO Why, 'tis not amiss, Pompey. Farewell. Go, say I 60
sent thee thither. For debt, Pompey? Or how?

ELBOW For being a bawd, for being a bawd.

LUCIO Well, then, imprison him. If imprisonment be the
due of a bawd, why, 'tis his right. Bawd is he doubtless,
and of antiquity too; bawd-born. Farewell, good
Pompey. Commend me to the prison, Pompey. You will
turn good husband now, Pompey. You will keep the
house.

POMPEY I hope, sir, your good worship will be my bail.

LUCIO No, indeed will I not, Pompey; it is not the wear. I 70
will pray, Pompey, to increase your bondage. If you
take it not patiently, why, your mettle is the more.
Adieu, trusty Pompey. Bless you, friar.

DUKE And you.

LUCIO Does Bridget paint still, Pompey, ha?

ELBOW Come your ways, sir, come.

POMPEY You will not bail me then, sir?

LUCIO Then, Pompey, nor now. What news abroad,
friar, what news?

ELBOW Come your ways, sir, come.   80

LUCIO Go to kennel, Pompey, go.

> *Exeunt Elbow, Pompey, and Officers*

What news, friar, of the Duke?

DUKE I know none. Can you tell me of any?

LUCIO Some say he is with the Emperor of Russia; other
some, he is in Rome. But where is he, think you?

DUKE I know not where, but wheresoever, I wish him
well.

LUCIO It was a mad fantastical trick of him to steal from

the state, and usurp the beggary he was never born to.

90 Lord Angelo dukes it well in his absence. He puts
transgression to't.

DUKE He does well in't.

LUCIO A little more lenity to lechery would do no harm
in him. Something too crabbed that way, friar.

DUKE It is too general a vice, and severity must cure it.

LUCIO Yes, in good sooth, the vice is of a great kindred.
It is well allied, but it is impossible to extirp it quite,
friar, till eating and drinking be put down. They say this
Angelo was not made by man and woman after this

100 downright way of creation. Is it true, think you?

DUKE How should he be made, then?

LUCIO Some report a sea-maid spawned him. Some that
he was begot between two stock-fishes. But it is certain
that when he makes water his urine is congealed ice.
That I know to be true. And he is a motion generative.
That's infallible.

DUKE You are pleasant, sir, and speak apace.

LUCIO Why, what a ruthless thing is this in him, for the
rebellion of a cod-piece to take away the life of a man!

110 Would the Duke that is absent have done this? Ere he
would have hanged a man for the getting a hundred
bastards, he would have paid for the nursing a thousand.
He had some feeling of the sport. He knew the service,
and that instructed him to mercy.

DUKE I never heard the absent Duke much detected for
women. He was not inclined that way.

LUCIO O, sir, you are deceived.

DUKE 'Tis not possible.

LUCIO Who? Not the Duke? Yes, your beggar of fifty,

120 and his use was to put a ducat in her clack-dish. The
Duke had crotchets in him. He would be drunk, too;
that let me inform you.

DUKE You do him wrong, surely.

LUCIO Sir, I was an inward of his. A shy fellow was the
Duke, and I believe I know the cause of his with-
drawing.

DUKE What, I prithee, might be the cause?

LUCIO No, pardon. 'Tis a secret must be locked within
the teeth and the lips. But this I can let you understand,
the greater file of the subject held the Duke to be wise. 130

DUKE Wise? Why, no question but he was.

LUCIO A very superficial, ignorant, unweighing fellow.

DUKE Either this is envy in you, folly, or mistaking. The
very stream of his life and the business he hath helmed
must, upon a warranted need, give him a better proclamation. Let him be but testimonied in his own bringings-
forth, and he shall appear to the envious a scholar, a
statesman, and a soldier. Therefore you speak unskilfully; or, if your knowledge be more, it is much
darkened in your malice. 140

LUCIO Sir, I know him, and I love him.

DUKE Love talks with better knowledge, and knowledge
with dearer love.

LUCIO Come, sir, I know what I know.

DUKE I can hardly believe that, since you know not what
you speak. But if ever the Duke return – as our prayers
are he may – let me desire you to make your answer
before him. If it be honest you have spoke, you have
courage to maintain it. I am bound to call upon you, and,
I pray you, your name? 150

LUCIO Sir, my name is Lucio, well known to the Duke.

DUKE He shall know you better, sir, if I may live to report
you.

LUCIO I fear you not.

DUKE O, you hope the Duke will return no more, or you
imagine me too unhurtful an opposite. But indeed I can

do you little harm; you'll forswear this again.

LUCIO I'll be hanged first. Thou art deceived in me, friar.
But no more of this. Canst thou tell if Claudio die to-
160 morrow or no?

DUKE Why should he die, sir?

LUCIO Why? For filling a bottle with a tun-dish. I would
the Duke we talk of were returned again. This ungenitured agent will unpeople the province with con-
tinency. Sparrows must not build in his house-eaves
because they are lecherous. The Duke yet would have
dark deeds darkly answered. He would never bring
them to light. Would he were returned. Marry, this
Claudio is condemned for untrussing. Farewell, good
170 friar. I prithee, pray for me. The Duke, I say to thee
again, would eat mutton on Fridays. He's not past it
yet, and I say to thee, he would mouth with a beggar,
though she smelt brown bread and garlic. Say that I
said so. Farewell. *Exit*

DUKE

No might nor greatness in mortality
Can censure 'scape; back-wounding calumny
The whitest virtue strikes. What king so strong
Can tie the gall up in the slanderous tongue?
But who comes here?

*Enter Escalus, Provost, and Officers with Mistress
Overdone*

180 ESCALUS Go! Away with her to prison.

MISTRESS OVERDONE Good my lord, be good to me.
Your honour is accounted a merciful man, good my
lord.

ESCALUS Double and treble admonition, and still forfeit
in the same kind? This would make mercy swear, and
play the tyrant.

PROVOST A bawd of eleven years' continuance, may it please your honour.

MISTRESS OVERDONE My lord, this is one Lucio's information against me. Mistress Kate Keepdown was 190 with child by him in the Duke's time. He promised her marriage. His child is a year and a quarter old, come Philip and Jacob. I have kept it myself, and see how he goes about to abuse me.

ESCALUS That fellow is a fellow of much licence. Let him be called before us. Away with her to prison. Go to, no more words.   *Exeunt Officers with Mistress Overdone*
Provost, my brother Angelo will not be altered. Claudio must die tomorrow. Let him be furnished with divines, and have all charitable preparation. If my brother 200 wrought by my pity, it should not be so with him.

PROVOST So please you, this friar hath been with him, and advised him for th'entertainment of death.

ESCALUS Good even, good father.

DUKE Bliss and goodness on you!

ESCALUS Of whence are you?

DUKE
Not of this country, though my chance is now
To use it for my time. I am a brother
Of gracious order, late come from the See,
In special business from his Holiness.   210

ESCALUS What news abroad i'th'world?

DUKE None, but that there is so great a fever on goodness that the dissolution of it must cure it. Novelty is only in request, and it is as dangerous to be aged in any kind of course as it is virtuous to be constant in any under- taking. There is scarce truth enough alive to make societies secure, but security enough to make fellow- ships accursed. Much upon this riddle runs the wisdom

of the world. This news is old enough, yet it is every
220 day's news. I pray you, sir, of what disposition was the
Duke?

ESCALUS One that, above all other strifes, contended
especially to know himself.

DUKE What pleasure was he given to?

ESCALUS Rather rejoicing to see another merry than
merry at anything which professed to make him rejoice:
a gentleman of all temperance. But leave we him to his
events, with a prayer they may prove prosperous, and
let me desire to know how you find Claudio prepared.
230 I am made to understand that you have lent him visita-
tion.

DUKE He professes to have received no sinister measure
from his judge, but most willingly humbles himself
to the determination of justice. Yet had he framed to
himself, by the instruction of his frailty, many deceiving
promises of life, which I, by my good leisure, have dis-
credited to him, and now is he resolved to die.

ESCALUS You have paid the heavens your function, and
the prisoner the very debt of your calling. I have
240 laboured for the poor gentleman to the extremest shore
of my modesty, but my brother-justice have I found so
severe that he hath forced me to tell him he is indeed
Justice.

DUKE If his own life answer the straitness of his proceed-
ing, it shall become him well; wherein if he chance to
fail, he hath sentenced himself.

ESCALUS I am going to visit the prisoner. Fare you well.

DUKE Peace be with you!

Exeunt Escalus and Provost

He who the sword of heaven will bear
250 Should be as holy as severe;
Pattern in himself to know,

Grace to stand, and virtue go;
More nor less to others paying
Than by self-offences weighing.
Shame to him whose cruel striking
Kills for faults of his own liking.
Twice treble shame on Angelo,
To weed my vice and let his grow.
O, what may man within him hide,
Though angel on the outward side?   260
How may likeness made in crimes,
Making practice on the times,
To-draw with idle spiders' strings
Most ponderous and substantial things!
Craft against vice I must apply.
With Angelo tonight shall lie
His old betrothèd, but despised:
So disguise shall by th'disguised
Pay with falsehood, false exacting,
And perform an old contracting.   *Exit* 270

*

Enter Mariana, and Boy singing   IV.1
BOY (*sings*)
     Take, O take those lips away
        That so sweetly were forsworn;
     And those eyes, the break of day,
        Lights that do mislead the morn:
     But my kisses bring again, bring again;
     Seals of love, but sealed in vain, sealed in vain.
        Enter Duke as a friar
MARIANA
  Break off thy song, and haste thee quick away.

113

Here comes a man of comfort, whose advice
Hath often stilled my brawling discontent.   *Exit Boy*

10   I cry you mercy, sir, and well could wish
You had not found me here so musical.
Let me excuse me, and believe me so,
My mirth it much displeased, but pleased my woe.

DUKE

'Tis good, though music oft hath such a charm
To make bad good, and good provoke to harm.
I pray you tell me, hath anybody inquired for me here
today? Much upon this time have I promised here to
meet.

MARIANA You have not been inquired after. I have sat
20   here all day.

    Enter Isabella

DUKE I do constantly believe you. The time is come even
now. I shall crave your forbearance a little. May be I
will call upon you anon for some advantage to yourself.

MARIANA I am always bound to you.   *Exit*

DUKE

Very well met, and welcome.
What is the news from this good deputy?

ISABELLA

He hath a garden circummured with brick,
Whose western side is with a vineyard backed;
And to that vineyard is a planchèd gate,
30   That makes his opening with this bigger key.
This other doth command a little door
Which from the vineyard to the garden leads.
There have I made my promise,
Upon the heavy middle of the night,
To call upon him.

DUKE

But shall you on your knowledge find this way?

ISABELLA

    I have ta'en a due and wary note upon't.
    With whispering and most guilty diligence,
    In action all of precept, he did show me
    The way twice o'er.

DUKE   Are there no other tokens   40
    Between you 'greed concerning her observance?

ISABELLA

    No, none, but only a repair i'th'dark,
    And that I have possessed him my most stay
    Can be but brief. For I have made him know
    I have a servant comes with me along,
    That stays upon me, whose persuasion is
    I come about my brother.

DUKE   'Tis well borne up.
    I have not yet made known to Mariana
    A word of this. What ho, within. Come forth.
      Enter Mariana
    I pray you, be acquainted with this maid;   50
    She comes to do you good.

ISABELLA   I do desire the like.

DUKE

    Do you persuade yourself that I respect you?

MARIANA

    Good friar, I know you do, and so have found it.

DUKE

    Take then this your companion by the hand,
    Who hath a story ready for your ear.
    I shall attend your leisure, but make haste.
    The vaporous night approaches.

MARIANA

    Will't please you walk aside?
                  Exeunt Mariana and Isabella

DUKE

    O place and greatness, millions of false eyes
60   Are stuck upon thee. Volumes of report
    Run with these false and most contrarious quests
    Upon thy doings; thousand escapes of wit
    Make thee the father of their idle dream,
    And rack thee in their fancies.

      Enter Mariana and Isabella

                              Welcome, how agreed?

ISABELLA

    She'll take the enterprise upon her, father,
    If you advise it.

DUKE   It is not my consent,
    But my entreaty too.

ISABELLA   Little have you to say
    When you depart from him but, soft and low,
    'Remember now my brother.'

MARIANA   Fear me not.

DUKE

70   Nor, gentle daughter, fear you not at all.
    He is your husband on a pre-contract.
    To bring you thus together, 'tis no sin,
    Sith that the justice of your title to him
    Doth flourish the deceit. Come, let us go;
    Our corn's to reap, for yet our tilth's to sow.   *Exeunt*

IV.2   *Enter Provost and Pompey*

PROVOST Come hither, sirrah. Can you cut off a man's
head?

POMPEY If the man be a bachelor, sir, I can; but if he be a
married man, he's his wife's head, and I can never cut
off a woman's head.

PROVOST Come, sir, leave me your snatches, and yield

me a direct answer. Tomorrow morning are to die
Claudio and Barnardine. Here is in our prison a common executioner, who in his office lacks a helper. If you
will take it on you to assist him, it shall redeem you 10
from your gyves; if not, you shall have your full time
of imprisonment, and your deliverance with an unpitied whipping, for you have been a notorious bawd.

POMPEY Sir, I have been an unlawful bawd time out of
mind, but yet I will be content to be a lawful hangman.
I would be glad to receive some instruction from my
fellow partner.

PROVOST What ho, Abhorson! Where's Abhorson, there?
Enter Abhorson

ABHORSON Do you call, sir?

PROVOST Sirrah, here's a fellow will help you tomorrow 20
in your execution. If you think it meet, compound with
him by the year, and let him abide here with you; if
not, use him for the present and dismiss him. He cannot
plead his estimation with you. He hath been a bawd.

ABHORSON A bawd, sir? Fie upon him, he will discredit
our mystery.

PROVOST Go to, sir, you weigh equally. A feather will
turn the scale.   *Exit*

POMPEY Pray, sir, by your good favour – for surely, sir, a
good favour you have, but that you have a hanging 30
look – do you call, sir, your occupation a mystery?

ABHORSON Ay, sir, a mystery.

POMPEY Painting, sir, I have heard say, is a mystery, and
your whores, sir, being members of my occupation,
using painting, do prove my occupation a mystery. But
what mystery there should be in hanging, if I should be
hanged, I cannot imagine.

ABHORSON Sir, it is a mystery.

POMPEY Proof?

40 ABHORSON Every true man's apparel fits your thief. If it
be too little for your thief, your true man thinks it big
enough. If it be too big for your thief, your thief
thinks it little enough. So every true man's apparel
fits your thief.

Enter Provost

PROVOST Are you agreed?

POMPEY Sir, I will serve him, for I do find your hangman is a more penitent trade than your bawd. He doth
oftener ask forgiveness.

PROVOST You, sirrah, provide your block and your axe
50 tomorrow four o'clock.

ABHORSON Come, on, bawd. I will instruct thee in my
trade. Follow!

POMPEY I do desire to learn, sir, and I hope, if you have
occasion to use me for your own turn, you shall find me
yare. For truly, sir, for your kindness I owe you a good
turn.

PROVOST

Call hither Barnardine and Claudio.

Exeunt Pompey and Abhorson

Th'one has my pity; not a jot the other,
Being a murderer, though he were my brother.

Enter Claudio

60 Look, here's the warrant, Claudio, for thy death.
'Tis now dead midnight, and by eight tomorrow
Thou must be made immortal. Where's Barnardine?

CLAUDIO

As fast locked up in sleep as guiltless labour
When it lies starkly in the traveller's bones.
He will not wake.

PROVOST Who can do good on him?
Well, go, prepare yourself.

Knocking

But hark, what noise?
Heaven give your spirits comfort. *Exit Claudio*
By and by.
I hope it is some pardon or reprieve
For the most gentle Claudio.
    Enter Duke as a friar
Welcome, father.

DUKE
The best and wholesom'st spirits of the night   70
Envelop you, good provost. Who called here of late?

PROVOST
None since the curfew rung.

DUKE
Not Isabel?

PROVOST   No.

DUKE   They will then, ere't be long.

PROVOST
What comfort is for Claudio?

DUKE
There's some in hope.

PROVOST   It is a bitter deputy.

DUKE
Not so, not so; his life is paralleled
Even with the stroke and line of his great justice.
He doth with holy abstinence subdue
That in himself which he spurs on his power
To qualify in others. Were he mealed with that   80
Which he corrects, then were he tyrannous,
But this being so, he's just.
    Knocking
Now are they come.
    Exit Provost
This is a gentle provost; seldom when
The steelèd gaoler is the friend of men.

Knocking

How now? What noise? That spirit's possessed with
haste
That wounds th'unsisting postern with these strokes.
Enter Provost

PROVOST
There he must stay until the officer
Arise to let him in. He is called up.

DUKE
Have you no countermand for Claudio yet,
90 But he must die tomorrow?

PROVOST   None, sir, none.

DUKE
As near the dawning, provost, as it is,
You shall hear more ere morning.

PROVOST   Happily
You something know, yet I believe there comes
No countermand; no such example have we.
Besides, upon the very siege of justice,
Lord Angelo hath to the public ear
Professed the contrary.
Enter a Messenger

DUKE This is his lordship's man.

PROVOST And here comes Claudio's pardon.

100 MESSENGER My lord hath sent you this note, and by me
this further charge: that you swerve not from the smallest
article of it, neither in time, matter, or other circumstance. Good morrow; for, as I take it, it is almost day.

PROVOST I shall obey him.   *Exit Messenger*

DUKE (*aside*)
This is his pardon, purchased by such sin
For which the pardoner himself is in:
Hence hath offence his quick celerity,
When it is borne in high authority.

When vice makes mercy, mercy's so extended
That for the fault's love is th'offender friended.   110
Now, sir, what news?

PROVOST I told you. Lord Angelo, belike thinking me re-
miss in mine office, awakens me with this unwonted
putting on – methinks strangely, for he hath not used
it before.

DUKE Pray you, let's hear.

PROVOST (reads the letter) *Whatsoever you may hear to the
contrary, let Claudio be executed by four of the clock, and,
in the afternoon, Barnardine. For my better satisfaction,
let me have Claudio's head sent me by five. Let this be*   120
*duly performed, with a thought that more depends on it
than we must yet deliver. Thus fail not to do your office,
as you will answer it at your peril.*
What say you to this, sir?

DUKE What is that Barnardine who is to be executed in
th'afternoon?

PROVOST A Bohemian born, but here nursed up and
bred. One that is a prisoner nine years old.

DUKE How came it that the absent Duke had not either
delivered him to his liberty or executed him? I have   130
heard it was ever his manner to do so.

PROVOST His friends still wrought reprieves for him;
and, indeed, his fact, till now in the government of Lord
Angelo, came not to an undoubtful proof.

DUKE It is now apparent?

PROVOST Most manifest, and not denied by himself.

DUKE Hath he borne himself penitently in prison? How
seems he to be touched?

PROVOST A man that apprehends death no more dread-
fully but as a drunken sleep; careless, reckless, and   140
fearless of what's past, present, or to come; insensible
of mortality, and desperately mortal.

DUKE He wants advice.

PROVOST He will hear none. He hath evermore had the liberty of the prison. Give him leave to escape hence, he would not. Drunk many times a day, if not many days entirely drunk. We have very oft awaked him, as if to carry him to execution, and showed him a seeming warrant for it. It hath not moved him at all.

150 DUKE More of him anon. There is written in your brow, provost, honesty and constancy. If I read it not truly, my ancient skill beguiles me; but in the boldness of my cunning I will lay myself in hazard. Claudio, whom here you have warrant to execute, is no greater forfeit to the law than Angelo who hath sentenced him. To make you understand this in a manifested effect, I crave but four days' respite, for the which you are to do me both a present and a dangerous courtesy.

PROVOST Pray, sir, in what?

160 DUKE In the delaying death.

PROVOST Alack, how may I do it, having the hour limited, and an express command, under penalty, to deliver his head in the view of Angelo? I may make my case as Claudio's, to cross this in the smallest.

DUKE By the vow of mine order I warrant you, if my instructions may be your guide. Let this Barnardine be this morning executed, and his head borne to Angelo.

PROVOST Angelo hath seen them both, and will discover the favour.

170 DUKE O, death's a great disguiser, and you may add to it. Shave the head, and tie the beard, and say it was the desire of the penitent to be so bared before his death. You know the course is common. If anything fall to you upon this, more than thanks and good fortune, by the saint whom I profess, I will plead against it with my life.

PROVOST Pardon me, good father, it is against my oath.

DUKE Were you sworn to the Duke or to the deputy?

PROVOST To him, and to his substitutes.

DUKE You will think you have made no offence if the
Duke avouch the justice of your dealing?   180.

PROVOST But what likelihood is in that?

DUKE Not a resemblance, but a certainty. Yet since I see
you fearful, that neither my coat, integrity, nor persuasion can with ease attempt you, I will go further than
I meant, to pluck all fears out of you. Look you, sir,
here is the hand and seal of the Duke. You know the
character, I doubt not, and the signet is not strange to
you.

PROVOST I know them both.

DUKE The contents of this is the return of the Duke. You 190
shall anon over-read it at your pleasure, where you shall
find within these two days he will be here. This is a
thing that Angelo knows not, for he this very day
receives letters of strange tenor, perchance of the Duke's
death, perchance entering into some monastery, but by
chance nothing of what is writ. Look, th'unfolding star
calls up the shepherd. Put not yourself into amazement
how these things should be. All difficulties are but easy
when they are known. Call your executioner, and off
with Barnardine's head. I will give him a present   200
shrift and advise him for a better place. Yet you are
amazed, but this shall absolutely resolve you. Come
away, it is almost clear dawn.

Exit with Provost

Enter Pompey   IV.3

POMPEY I am as well acquainted here as I was in our
house of profession. One would think it were Mistress
Overdone's own house, for here be many of her old

customers. First, here's young Master Rash. He's in for
a commodity of brown paper and old ginger, nine-score
and seventeen pounds, of which he made five marks
ready money. Marry, then ginger was not much in request, or the old women were all dead. Then is there
here one Master Caper, at the suit of Master Threepile
the mercer, for some four suits of peach-coloured satin,
which now peaches him a beggar. Then have we here
young Dizzy, and young Master Deepvow, and Master
Copperspur, and Master Starve-lackey, the rapier and
dagger man, and young Drop-heir that killed lusty
Pudding, and Master Forthright the tilter, and brave
Master Shoe-tie the great traveller, and wild Half-can
that stabbed Pots, and I think forty more, all great doers
in our trade, and are now 'for the Lord's sake'.

Enter Abhorson

ABHORSON Sirrah, bring Barnardine hither.

POMPEY Master Barnardine, you must rise and be
hanged, Master Barnardine.

ABHORSON What ho, Barnardine!

BARNARDINE (*within*) A pox o' your throats! Who makes
that noise there? What are you?

POMPEY Your friends, sir, the hangman. You must be so
good, sir, to rise and be put to death.

BARNARDINE (*within*) Away, you rogue, away! I am
sleepy.

ABHORSON Tell him he must awake, and that quickly too.

POMPEY Pray, Master Barnardine, awake till you are
executed, and sleep afterwards.

ABHORSON Go in to him, and fetch him out.

POMPEY He is coming, sir, he is coming. I hear his straw
rustle.

Enter Barnardine

ABHORSON Is the axe upon the block, sirrah?

POMPEY Very ready, sir.

BARNARDINE How now, Abhorson, what's the news with you?

ABHORSON Truly, sir, I would desire you to clap into your prayers, for look you, the warrant's come.   40

BARNARDINE You rogue, I have been drinking all night. I am not fitted for't.

POMPEY O, the better, sir, for he that drinks all night, and is hanged betimes in the morning, may sleep the sounder all the next day.

Enter Duke as a friar

ABHORSON Look you, sir, here comes your ghostly father. Do we jest now, think you?

DUKE Sir, induced by my charity, and hearing how hastily you are to depart, I am come to advise you, comfort you, and pray with you.   50

BARNARDINE Friar, not I. I have been drinking hard all night and I will have more time to prepare me, or they shall beat out my brains with billets. I will not consent to die this day, that's certain.

DUKE O, sir, you must, and therefore I beseech you look forward on the journey you shall go.

BARNARDINE I swear I will not die today for any man's persuasion.

DUKE But hear you.

BARNARDINE Not a word. If you have anything to say to   60 me, come to my ward, for thence will not I today.   *Exit*

Enter Provost

DUKE

Unfit to live or die. O gravel heart!
After him, fellows: bring him to the block.

Exeunt Abhorson and Pompey

PROVOST

Now, sir, how do you find the prisoner?

DUKE

A creature unprepared, unmeet for death,
And to transport him in the mind he is
Were damnable.

PROVOST　　　　　Here in the prison, father,
There died this morning of a cruel fever
One Ragozine, a most notorious pirate,
70 A man of Claudio's years, his beard and head
Just of his colour. What if we do omit
This reprobate till he were well inclined,
And satisfy the deputy with the visage
Of Ragozine, more like to Claudio?

DUKE

O, 'tis an accident that heaven provides.
Dispatch it presently; the hour draws on
Prefixed by Angelo. See this be done,
And sent according to command, whiles I
Persuade this rude wretch willingly to die.

PROVOST

80 This shall be done, good father, presently,
But Barnardine must die this afternoon,
And how shall we continue Claudio,
To save me from the danger that might come
If he were known alive?

DUKE　　　　　　　　Let this be done.
Put them in secret holds, both Barnardine
And Claudio. Ere twice the sun hath made
His journal greeting to yond generation,
You shall find your safety manifested.

PROVOST

I am your free dependant.

DUKE

90 Quick, dispatch, and send the head to Angelo.

Exit Provost

126

Now will I write letters to Varrius –
The provost, he shall bear them – whose contents
Shall witness to him I am near at home,
And that by great injunctions I am bound
To enter publicly. Him I'll desire
To meet me at the consecrated fount
A league below the city, and from thence,
By cold gradation and well-balanced form,
We shall proceed with Angelo.
   Enter Provost

PROVOST
  Here is the head. I'll carry it myself.   100

DUKE
  Convenient is it. Make a swift return,
  For I would commune with you of such things
  That want no ear but yours.

PROVOST   I'll make all speed.   *Exit*

ISABELLA (*within*)
  Peace, ho, be here.

DUKE
  The tongue of Isabel. She's come to know
  If yet her brother's pardon be come hither,
  But I will keep her ignorant of her good,
  To make her heavenly comforts of despair
  When it is least expected.
    Enter Isabella

ISABELLA   Ho, by your leave!

DUKE
  Good morning to you, fair and gracious daughter.   110

ISABELLA
  The better, given me by so holy a man.
  Hath yet the deputy sent my brother's pardon?

DUKE
  He hath released him, Isabel, from the world.

His head is off and sent to Angelo.

ISABELLA

Nay, but it is not so.

DUKE

It is no other. Show your wisdom, daughter,
In your close patience.

ISABELLA

O, I will to him and pluck out his eyes!

DUKE

You shall not be admitted to his sight.

ISABELLA

120 Unhappy Claudio! Wretched Isabel!
Injurious world! Most damnèd Angelo!

DUKE

This nor hurts him nor profits you a jot;
Forbear it therefore, give your cause to heaven.
Mark what I say, which you shall find
By every syllable a faithful verity.
The Duke comes home tomorrow – nay, dry your eyes –
One of our covent, and his confessor,
Gives me this instance. Already he hath carried
Notice to Escalus and Angelo,
130 Who do prepare to meet him at the gates,
There to give up their power. If you can, pace your
            wisdom
In that good path that I would wish it go,
And you shall have your bosom on this wretch,
Grace of the Duke, revenges to your heart,
And general honour.

ISABELLA   I am directed by you.

DUKE

This letter then to Friar Peter give.
'Tis that he sent me of the Duke's return.
Say, by this token, I desire his company

At Mariana's house tonight. Her cause and yours
I'll perfect him withal, and he shall bring you   140
Before the Duke; and to the head of Angelo
Accuse him home and home. For my poor self,
I am combinèd by a sacred vow
And shall be absent. Wend you with this letter.
Command these fretting waters from your eyes
With a light heart. Trust not my holy order
If I pervert your course. Who's here?

Enter Lucio

LUCIO Good even. Friar, where's the provost?

DUKE Not within, sir.

LUCIO O pretty Isabella, I am pale at mine heart to see 150
thine eyes so red. Thou must be patient. I am fain to
dine and sup with water and bran. I dare not for my
head fill my belly; one fruitful meal would set me to't.
But they say the Duke will be here tomorrow. By my
troth, Isabel, I loved thy brother. If the old fantastical
Duke of dark corners had been at home, he had lived.

Exit Isabella

DUKE Sir, the Duke is marvellous little beholding to your
reports, but the best is, he lives not in them.

LUCIO Friar, thou knowest not the Duke so well as I do.
He's a better woodman than thou tak'st him for.   160

DUKE Well, you'll answer this one day. Fare ye well.

LUCIO Nay, tarry, I'll go along with thee. I can tell thee
pretty tales of the Duke.

DUKE You have told me too many of him already, sir, if
they be true; if not true, none were enough.

LUCIO I was once before him for getting a wench with
child.

DUKE Did you such a thing?

LUCIO Yes, marry, did I, but I was fain to forswear it.
They would else have married me to the rotten medlar. 170

DUKE Sir, your company is fairer than honest. Rest you
well.

LUCIO By my troth, I'll go with thee to the lane's end. If
bawdy talk offend you, we'll have very little of it. Nay,
friar, I am a kind of burr, I shall stick.   *Exeunt*

IV.4   *Enter Angelo and Escalus*

ESCALUS Every letter he hath writ hath disvouched other.

ANGELO In most uneven and distracted manner. His
actions show much like to madness. Pray heaven his
wisdom be not tainted. And why meet him at the gates,
and reliver our authorities there?

ESCALUS I guess not.

ANGELO And why should we proclaim it in an hour before
his entering, that if any crave redress of injustice, they
should exhibit their petitions in the street?

10 ESCALUS He shows his reason for that – to have a dispatch
of complaints, and to deliver us from devices hereafter,
which shall then have no power to stand against us.

ANGELO   .

Well, I beseech you let it be proclaimed.
Betimes i'th'morn I'll call you at your house.
Give notice to such men of sort and suit
As are to meet him.

ESCALUS   I shall, sir. Fare you well.

ANGELO

Good night.   *Exit Escalus*

This deed unshapes me quite, makes me unpregnant
And dull to all proceedings. A deflowered maid,

20   And by an eminent body that enforced
The law against it! But that her tender shame
Will not proclaim against her maiden loss,
How might she tongue me? Yet reason dares her no,

For my authority bears a credent bulk
That no particular scandal once can touch
But it confounds the breather. He should have lived,
Save that his riotous youth with dangerous sense
Might in the times to come have ta'en revenge,
By so receiving a dishonoured life
With ransom of such shame. Would yet he had lived.   30
Alack, when once our grace we have forgot,
Nothing goes right. We would, and we would not.

Exit

Enter Duke, in his own habit, and Friar Peter   IV.5

DUKE
These letters at fit time deliver me.
The provost knows our purpose and our plot.
The matter being afoot, keep your instruction,
And hold you ever to our special drift,
Though sometimes you do blench from this to that,
As cause doth minister. Go call at Flavius' house,
And tell him where I stay. Give the like notice
To Valentius, Rowland, and to Crassus,
And bid them bring the trumpets to the gate;
But send me Flavius first.

FRIAR PETER   It shall be speeded well.   10

Exit

Enter Varrius

DUKE
I thank thee, Varrius, thou hast made good haste.
Come, we will walk. There's other of our friends
Will greet us here anon, my gentle Varrius.   *Exeunt*

Enter Isabella and Mariana

ISABELLA

To speak so indirectly I am loath.
I would say the truth, but to accuse him so,
That is your part. Yet I am advised to do it,
He says, to veil full purpose.

MARIANA   Be ruled by him.

ISABELLA

Besides, he tells me that if peradventure
He speak against me on the adverse side,
I should not think it strange, for 'tis a physic
That's bitter to sweet end.

MARIANA

I would Friar Peter –

            Enter Friar Peter

ISABELLA   O, peace, the friar is come.

FRIAR PETER

10   Come, I have found you out a stand most fit,
Where you may have such vantage on the Duke
He shall not pass you. Twice have the trumpets
            sounded.
The generous and gravest citizens
Have hent the gates, and very near upon
The Duke is entering. Therefore hence, away. *Exeunt*

*

V.1   *Enter Duke, Varrius, Lords, Angelo, Escalus, Lucio,
            Provost, Officers, and Citizens at several doors*

DUKE

My very worthy cousin, fairly met.
Our old and faithful friend, we are glad to see you.

ANGELO *and* ESCALUS

Happy return be to your royal grace.

DUKE

  Many and hearty thankings to you both.
  We have made inquiry of you, and we hear
  Such goodness of your justice that our soul
  Cannot but yield you forth to public thanks,
  Forerunning more requital.

ANGELO   You make my bonds still greater.

DUKE

  O, your desert speaks loud, and I should wrong it
  To lock it in the wards of covert bosom,   10
  When it deserves with characters of brass
  A forted residence 'gainst the tooth of time
  And razure of oblivion. Give me your hand,
  And let the subject see, to make them know
  That outward courtesies would fain proclaim
  Favours that keep within. Come, Escalus,
  You must walk by us on our other hand,
  And good supporters are you.

    Enter Friar Peter and Isabella

FRIAR PETER

  Now is your time. Speak loud and kneel before him.

ISABELLA

  Justice, O royal Duke! Vail your regard   20
  Upon a wronged – I would fain have said, a maid.
  O worthy prince, dishonour not your eye
  By throwing it on any other object
  Till you have heard me in my true complaint
  And given me justice, justice, justice, justice!

DUKE

  Relate your wrongs. In what? By whom? Be brief.
  Here is Lord Angelo shall give you justice.
  Reveal yourself to him.

ISABELLA   O worthy Duke,
  You bid me seek redemption of the devil.

30 Hear me yourself, for that which I must speak
Must either punish me, not being believed,
Or wring redress from you. Hear me, O hear me, hear.

ANGELO
My lord, her wits, I fear me, are not firm.
She hath been a suitor to me for her brother,
Cut off by course of justice –

ISABELLA   By course of justice!

ANGELO
And she will speak most bitterly and strange.

ISABELLA
Most strange, but yet most truly, will I speak.
That Angelo's forsworn, is it not strange?
That Angelo's a murderer, is't not strange?
40 That Angelo is an adulterous thief,
An hypocrite, a virgin-violator,
Is it not strange, and strange?

DUKE   Nay, it is ten times strange.

ISABELLA
It is not truer he is Angelo
Than this is all as true as it is strange.
Nay, it is ten times true, for truth is truth
To th'end of reck'ning.

DUKE   Away with her. Poor soul,
She speaks this in th'infirmity of sense.

ISABELLA
O prince, I conjure thee, as thou believ'st
There is another comfort than this world,
50 That thou neglect me not with that opinion
That I am touched with madness. Make not impossible
That which but seems unlike. 'Tis not impossible
But one, the wicked'st caitiff on the ground,
May seem as shy, as grave, as just, as absolute
As Angelo. Even so may Angelo,

134

In all his dressings, characts, titles, forms,
Be an arch-villain. Believe it, royal prince.
If he be less, he's nothing: but he's more,
Had I more name for badness.

DUKE   By mine honesty,
If she be mad, as I believe no other,   60
Her madness hath the oddest frame of sense,
Such a dependency of thing on thing,
As e'er I heard in madness.

ISABELLA   O gracious Duke,
Harp not on that, nor do not banish reason
For inequality, but let your reason serve
To make the truth appear where it seems hid,
And hide the false seems true.

DUKE   Many that are not mad
Have sure more lack of reason. What would you say?

ISABELLA
I am the sister of one Claudio,
Condemned upon the act of fornication   70
To lose his head, condemned by Angelo.
I, in probation of a sisterhood,
Was sent to by my brother. One Lucio
As then the messenger –

LUCIO   That's I, an't like your grace.
I came to her from Claudio, and desired her
To try her gracious fortune with Lord Angelo
For her poor brother's pardon.

ISABELLA   That's he indeed.

DUKE
You were not bid to speak.

LUCIO   No, my good lord,
Nor wished to hold my peace.

DUKE   I wish you now, then.
Pray you, take note of it, and when you have   80

135

A business for yourself, pray heaven you then
Be perfect.

LUCIO   I warrant your honour.

DUKE

The warrant's for yourself: take heed to't.

ISABELLA

This gentleman told somewhat of my tale.

LUCIO

Right.

DUKE

It may be right, but you are i'the wrong
To speak before your time. Proceed.

ISABELLA   I went
To this pernicious caitiff deputy –

DUKE

That's somewhat madly spoken.

ISABELLA   Pardon it,
90 The phrase is to the matter.

DUKE

Mended again. The matter. Proceed.

ISABELLA

In brief, to set the needless process by,
How I persuaded, how I prayed, and kneeled,
How he refelled me, and how I replied –
For this was of much length – the vile conclusion
I now begin with grief and shame to utter.
He would not, but by gift of my chaste body
To his concup'scible intemperate lust,
Release my brother, and after much debatement
100 My sisterly remorse confutes mine honour,
And I did yield to him. But the next morn betimes,
His purpose surfeiting, he sends a warrant
For my poor brother's head.

DUKE   This is most likely!

ISABELLA

O, that it were as like as it is true.

DUKE

By heaven, fond wretch, thou know'st not what thou
    speak'st,
Or else thou art suborned against his honour
In hateful practice. First, his integrity
Stands without blemish. Next, it imports no reason
That with such vehemency he should pursue
Faults proper to himself. If he had so offended,   110
He would have weighed thy brother by himself,
And not have cut him off. Someone hath set you on.
Confess the truth, and say by whose advice
Thou cam'st here to complain.   And is this all?

ISABELLA

Then, O you blessèd ministers above,
Keep me in patience, and with ripened time
Unfold the evil which is here wrapped up
In countenance. Heaven shield your grace from woe,
As I thus wronged hence unbelievèd go.

DUKE

I know you'd fain be gone. An officer!   120
To prison with her. Shall we thus permit
A blasting and a scandalous breath to fall
On him so near us? This needs must be a practice.
Who knew of your intent and coming hither?

ISABELLA

One that I would were here, Friar Lodowick.

DUKE

A ghostly father, belike. Who knows that Lodowick?

LUCIO

My lord, I know him, 'tis a meddling friar;
I do not like the man. Had he been lay, my lord,
For certain words he spake against your grace

130   In your retirement I had swinged him soundly.

DUKE

    Words against me? This' a good friar, belike,
    And to set on this wretched woman here
    Against our substitute! Let this friar be found.

LUCIO

    But yesternight, my lord, she and that friar,
    I saw them at the prison. A saucy friar,
    A very scurvy fellow.

FRIAR PETER

    Blessed be your royal grace,
    I have stood by, my lord, and I have heard
    Your royal ear abused. First hath this woman
140   Most wrongfully accused your substitute,
    Who is as free from touch or soil with her
    As she from one ungot.

DUKE   We did believe no less.
    Know you that Friar Lodowick that she speaks of?

FRIAR PETER

    I know him for a man divine and holy,
    Not scurvy, nor a temporary meddler,
    As he's reported by this gentleman,
    And, on my trust, a man that never yet
    Did – as he vouches – misreport your grace.

LUCIO

    My lord, most villainously, believe it.

FRIAR PETER

150   Well, he in time may come to clear himself,
    But at this instant he is sick, my lord,
    Of a strange fever. Upon his mere request,
    Being come to knowledge that there was complaint
    Intended 'gainst Lord Angelo, came I hither,
    To speak, as from his mouth, what he doth know
    Is true and false, and what he with his oath

And all probation will make up full clear,
Whensoever he's convented. First, for this woman,
To justify this worthy nobleman,
So vulgarly and personally accused,   160
Her shall you hear disprovèd to her eyes,
Till she herself confess it.

DUKE   Good friar, let's hear it.

Isabella is led off, guarded

Enter Mariana

Do you not smile at this, Lord Angelo?
O heaven, the vanity of wretched fools!
Give us some seats. Come, cousin Angelo,
In this I'll be impartial. Be you judge
Of your own cause. Is this the witness, friar?
First, let her show her face, and after speak.

MARIANA
Pardon, my lord, I will not show my face
Until my husband bid me.   170

DUKE What, are you married?

MARIANA No, my lord.

DUKE Are you a maid?

MARIANA No, my lord.

DUKE A widow, then?

MARIANA Neither, my lord.

DUKE Why, you are nothing then. Neither maid, widow,
nor wife?

LUCIO My lord, she may be a punk. For many of them are
neither maid, widow, nor wife.   180

DUKE
Silence that fellow. I would he had some cause
To prattle for himself.

LUCIO Well, my lord.

MARIANA
My lord, I do confess I ne'er was married,

And I confess besides I am no maid;
I have known my husband, yet my husband
Knows not that ever he knew me.

LUCIO He was drunk, then, my lord. It can be no better.

DUKE For the benefit of silence, would thou wert so too.

190 LUCIO Well, my lord.

DUKE

This is no witness for Lord Angelo.

MARIANA

Now I come to't, my lord:
She that accuses him of fornication
In selfsame manner doth accuse my husband;
And charges him, my lord, with such a time
When, I'll depose, I had him in mine arms,
With all th'effect of love.

ANGELO

Charges she more than me?

MARIANA   Not that I know.

DUKE

No? You say your husband?

MARIANA

200 Why, just, my lord, and that is Angelo,
Who thinks he knows that he ne'er knew my body,
But knows, he thinks, that he knows Isabel's.

ANGELO

This is a strange abuse. Let's see thy face.

MARIANA

My husband bids me. Now I will unmask.
     She unveils
This is that face, thou cruel Angelo,
Which once thou swor'st was worth the looking on.
This is the hand which, with a vowed contract,
Was fast belocked in thine. This is the body
That took away the match from Isabel,

And did supply thee at thy garden-house   210
In her imagined person.

DUKE   Know you this woman?

LUCIO
Carnally, she says.

DUKE   Sirrah, no more!

LUCIO
Enough, my lord.

ANGELO
My lord, I must confess I know this woman,
And five years since there was some speech of marriage
Betwixt myself and her, which was broke off,
Partly for that her promisèd proportions
Came short of composition, but in chief
For that her reputation was disvalued
In levity; since which time of five years   220
I never spake with her, saw her, nor heard from her,
Upon my faith and honour.

MARIANA   Noble prince,
As there comes light from heaven and words from
          breath,
As there is sense in truth and truth in virtue,
I am affianced this man's wife as strongly
As words could make up vows, and, my good lord,
But Tuesday night last gone in's garden-house
He knew me as a wife. As this is true,
Let me in safety raise me from my knees
Or else forever be confixèd here   230
A marble monument.

ANGELO   I did but smile till now.
Now, good my lord, give me the scope of justice.
My patience here is touched. I do perceive
These poor informal women are no more
But instruments of some more mightier member

That sets them on. Let me have way, my lord,
To find this practice out.

DUKE   Ay, with my heart,
And punish them to your height of pleasure.
Thou foolish friar, and thou pernicious woman,
240 Compact with her that's gone, think'st thou thy oaths,
Though they would swear down each particular saint,
Were testimonies against his worth and credit
That's sealed in approbation? You, Lord Escalus,
Sit with my cousin, lend him your kind pains
To find out this abuse, whence 'tis derived.
There is another friar that set them on;
Let him be sent for.

FRIAR PETER

Would he were here, my lord, for he indeed
Hath set the women on to this complaint.
250 Your provost knows the place where he abides
And he may fetch him.

DUKE   Go do it instantly;

Exit Provost

And you, my noble and well-warranted cousin,
Whom it concerns to hear this matter forth,
Do with your injuries as seems you best,
In any chastisement. I for a while
Will leave, but stir not you till you have well
Determinèd upon these slanderers.

ESCALUS

My lord, we'll do it throughly.   *Exit Duke*
Signor Lucio, did not you say you knew that Friar
260 Lodowick to be a dishonest person?

LUCIO *Cucullus non facit monachum.* Honest in nothing
but in his clothes, and one that hath spoke most vil-
lainous speeches of the Duke.

ESCALUS We shall entreat you to abide here till he come

and enforce them against him. We shall find this friar a
notable fellow.

LUCIO As any in Vienna, on my word.

ESCALUS Call that same Isabel here once again. I would
speak with her.   *Exit an Attendant*
Pray you, my lord, give me leave to question. You shall 270
see how I'll handle her.

LUCIO Not better than he, by her own report.

ESCALUS Say you?

LUCIO Marry, sir, I think, if you handled her privately,
she would sooner confess. Perchance publicly she'll be
ashamed.

> *Enter Duke, as a friar, Provost, Isabella, and*
> *Officers*

ESCALUS I will go darkly to work with her.

LUCIO That's the way, for women are light at midnight.

ESCALUS Come on, mistress, here's a gentlewoman
denies all that you have said.   280

LUCIO My lord, here comes the rascal I spoke of – here
with the provost.

ESCALUS In very good time. Speak not you to him, till we
call upon you.

LUCIO Mum.

ESCALUS Come, sir, did you set these women on to
slander Lord Angelo? They have confessed you did.

DUKE 'Tis false.

ESCALUS How? Know you where you are?

DUKE
Respect to your great place, and let the devil   290
Be sometime honoured for his burning throne.
Where is the Duke? 'Tis he should hear me speak.

ESCALUS
The Duke's in us, and we will hear you speak.
Look you speak justly.

143

DUKE
Boldly at least. But O, poor souls,
Come you to seek the lamb here of the fox?
Good night to your redress. Is the Duke gone?
Then is your cause gone too. The Duke's unjust,
Thus to retort your manifest appeal
300 And put your trial in the villain's mouth
Which here you come to accuse.

LUCIO
This is the rascal. This is he I spoke of.

ESCALUS
Why, thou unreverend and unhallowed friar,
Is't not enough thou hast suborned these women
To accuse this worthy man but, in foul mouth,
And in the witness of his proper ear,
To call him villain? And then to glance from him
To th'Duke himself, to tax him with injustice?
Take him hence. To th'rack with him. We'll touse you
310 Joint by joint, but we will know his purpose.
What? Unjust?

DUKE   Be not so hot. The Duke
Dare no more stretch this finger of mine than he
Dare rack his own. His subject am I not,
Nor here provincial. My business in this state
Made me a looker-on here in Vienna,
Where I have seen corruption boil and bubble
Till it o'errun the stew. Laws for all faults,
But faults so countenanced that the strong statutes
Stand like the forfeits in a barber's shop,
320 As much in mock as mark.

ESCALUS
Slander to th'state. Away with him to prison.

ANGELO
What can you vouch against him, Signor Lucio?

144

Is this the man that you did tell us of?

LUCIO 'Tis he, my lord. Come hither, goodman baldpate.
Do you know me?

DUKE I remember you, sir, by the sound of your voice. I
met you at the prison in the absence of the Duke.

LUCIO O, did you so? And do you remember what you
said of the Duke?

DUKE Most notedly, sir.   330

LUCIO Do you so, sir? And was the Duke a fleshmonger, a
fool, and a coward, as you then reported him to be?

DUKE You must, sir, change persons with me, ere you
make that my report. You, indeed, spoke so of him, and
much more, much worse.

LUCIO O thou damnable fellow, did not I pluck thee by
the nose for thy speeches?

DUKE I protest I love the Duke as I love myself.

ANGELO Hark how the villain would close now, after his
treasonable abuses.   340

ESCALUS Such a fellow is not to be talked withal. Away
with him to prison. Where is the provost? Away with
him to prison. Lay bolts enough upon him. Let him
speak no more. Away with those giglots too, and with
the other confederate companion.

The Provost lays hands on the Duke

DUKE Stay, sir, stay a while.

ANGELO What, resists he? Help him, Lucio.

LUCIO Come, sir, come, sir, come, sir! Foh, sir! Why, you
bald-pated, lying rascal, you must be hooded, must you?
Show your knave's visage, with a pox to you. Show   350
your sheep-biting face, and be hanged an hour. Will't
not off?

He pulls off the Friar's hood, and discovers the Duke

DUKE
Thou art the first knave that e'er mad'st a duke.

First, provost, let me bail these gentle three –
(*to Lucio*) Sneak not away, sir, for the friar and you
Must have a word anon. Lay hold on him.

LUCIO

This may prove worse than hanging.

DUKE (*to Escalus*)

What you have spoke I pardon. Sit you down.
We'll borrow place of him. (*To Angelo*) Sir, by your
  leave.
360 Hast thou or word, or wit, or impudence
That yet can do thee office? If thou hast,
Rely upon it till my tale be heard,
And hold no longer out.

ANGELO   O my dread lord,
I should be guiltier than my guiltiness
To think I can be undiscernible,
When I perceive your grace, like power divine,
Hath looked upon my passes. Then, good prince,
No longer session hold upon my shame,
But let my trial be mine own confession.
370 Immediate sentence, then, and sequent death
Is all the grace I beg.

DUKE   Come hither, Mariana.
Say, wast thou e'er contracted to this woman?

ANGELO

I was, my lord.

DUKE

Go take her hence, and marry her instantly.
Do you the office, friar, which consummate,
Return him here again. Go with him, provost.
    Exit Angelo, with Mariana, Friar Peter, and Provost

ESCALUS

My lord, I am more amazed at his dishonour
Than at the strangeness of it.

DUKE   Come hither, Isabel.
 Your friar is now your prince. As I was then
 Advertising and holy to your business,   380
 Not changing heart with habit, I am still
 Attorneyed at your service.

ISABELLA   O, give me pardon,
 That I, your vassal, have employed and pained
 Your unknown sovereignty.

DUKE   You are pardoned, Isabel.
 And now, dear maid, be you as free to us.
 Your brother's death, I know, sits at your heart,
 And you may marvel why I obscured myself,
 Labouring to save his life, and would not rather
 Make rash remonstrance of my hidden power
 Than let him so be lost. O most kind maid, 390
 It was the swift celerity of his death,
 Which I did think with slower foot came on,
 That brained my purpose; but peace be with him.
 That life is better life past fearing death
 Than that which lives to fear. Make it your comfort,
 So happy is your brother.

  Enter Angelo, Mariana, Friar Peter, Provost

ISABELLA   I do, my lord.

DUKE
 For this new-married man approaching here,
 Whose salt imagination yet hath wronged
 Your well-defended honour, you must pardon
 For Mariana's sake, but as he adjudged your brother, 400
 Being criminal, in double violation
 Of sacred chastity, and of promise-breach,
 Thereon dependent, for your brother's life,
 The very mercy of the law cries out
 Most audible, even from his proper tongue,
 'An Angelo for Claudio, death for death!'

Haste still pays haste, and leisure answers leisure,
Like doth quit like, and Measure still for Measure.
Then, Angelo, thy faults thus manifested,
410 Which, though thou wouldst deny, denies thee vantage,
We do condemn thee to the very block
Where Claudio stooped to death, and with like haste.
Away with him.

MARIANA   O, my most gracious lord,
I hope you will not mock me with a husband.

DUKE
It is your husband mocked you with a husband.
Consenting to the safeguard of your honour
I thought your marriage fit; else imputation,
For that he knew you, might reproach your life
And choke your good to come. For his possessions,
420 Although by confiscation they are ours,
We do instate and widow you with all,
To buy you a better husband.

MARIANA   O my dear lord,
I crave no other, nor no better man.

DUKE
Never crave him. We are definitive.

MARIANA
Gentle my liege! –

DUKE   You do but lose your labour.
Away with him to death. (*To Lucio*) Now, sir, to you.

MARIANA
O my good lord! Sweet Isabel, take my part,
Lend me your knees, and, all my life to come,
I'll lend you all my life to do you service.

DUKE
430 Against all sense you do importune her.
Should she kneel down in mercy of this fact,
Her brother's ghost his pavèd bed would break,

And take her hence in horror.

MARIANA   Isabel,
Sweet Isabel, do yet but kneel by me.
Hold up your hands, say nothing, I'll speak all.
They say best men are moulded out of faults,
And, for the most, become much more the better
For being a little bad. So may my husband.
O Isabel, will you not lend a knee?

DUKE
He dies for Claudio's death.

ISABELLA (*kneeling*)   Most bounteous sir,   440
Look, if it please you, on this man condemned
As if my brother lived. I partly think
A due sincerity governèd his deeds
Till he did look on me. Since it is so,
Let him not die. My brother had but justice,
In that he did the thing for which he died.
For Angelo,
His act did not o'ertake his bad intent,
And must be buried but as an intent
That perished by the way. Thoughts are no subjects,   450
Intents but merely thoughts.

MARIANA   Merely, my lord.

DUKE
Your suit's unprofitable. Stand up, I say.
I have bethought me of another fault.
Provost, how came it Claudio was beheaded
At an unusual hour?

PROVOST   It was commanded so.

DUKE
Had you a special warrant for the deed?

PROVOST
No, my good lord, it was by private message.

149

DUKE

    For which I do discharge you of your office;

    Give up your keys.

PROVOST   Pardon me, noble lord,

460   I thought it was a fault, but knew it not,

    Yet did repent me after more advice,

    For testimony whereof, one in the prison

    That should by private order else have died

    I have reserved alive.

DUKE   What's he?

PROVOST   His name is Barnardine.

DUKE

    I would thou hadst done so by Claudio.

    Go, fetch him hither. Let me look upon him.

                          Exit Provost

ESCALUS

    I am sorry one so learned and so wise

    As you, Lord Angelo, have still appeared,

    Should slip so grossly, both in the heat of blood

470   And lack of tempered judgement afterward.

ANGELO

    I am sorry that such sorrow I procure,

    And so deep sticks it in my penitent heart

    That I crave death more willingly than mercy.

    'Tis my deserving, and I do entreat it.

        Enter Barnardine and Provost, Claudio blindfold,

        Juliet

DUKE Which is that Barnardine?

PROVOST   This, my lord.

DUKE

    There was a friar told me of this man.

    Sirrah, thou art said to have a stubborn soul,

    That apprehends no further than this world,

    And squar'st thy life according. Thou'rt condemned,

480 But, for those earthly faults, I quit them all,
And pray thee take this mercy to provide
For better times to come. Friar, advise him:
I leave him to your hand. What muffled fellow's that?

PROVOST
This is another prisoner that I saved,
Who should have died when Claudio lost his head,
As like almost to Claudio as himself.

He unmuffles Claudio

DUKE (*to Isabella*)
If he be like your brother, for his sake
Is he pardoned, and for your lovely sake,
Give me your hand and say you will be mine.
490 He is my brother too. But fitter time for that.
By this Lord Angelo perceives he's safe;
Methinks I see a quickening in his eye.
Well, Angelo, your evil quits you well.
Look that you love your wife, her worth worth yours.
I find an apt remission in myself,
And yet here's one in place I cannot pardon.
(*To Lucio*) You, sirrah, that knew me for a fool, a coward,
One all of luxury, an ass, a madman,
Wherein have I so deserved of you,
500 That you extol me thus?

LUCIO 'Faith, my lord, I spoke it but according to the
trick. If you will hang me for it, you may. But I had
rather it would please you I might be whipped.

DUKE
Whipped first, sir, and hanged after.
Proclaim it, provost, round about the city,
If any woman wronged by this lewd fellow –
As I have heard him swear himself there's one
Whom he begot with child – let her appear,
And he shall marry her. The nuptial finished,

510 Let him be whipped and hanged.

LUCIO I beseech your highness, do not marry me to a
whore. Your highness said even now, I made you a
duke. Good my lord, do not recompense me in making
me a cuckold.

DUKE

Upon mine honour, thou shalt marry her.

Thy slanders I forgive, and therewithal

Remit thy other forfeits. Take him to prison,

And see our pleasure herein executed.

LUCIO Marrying a punk, my lord, is pressing to death,
520 whipping, and hanging.

DUKE

Slandering a prince deserves it.

Exeunt Officers with Lucio

She, Claudio, that you wronged, look you restore.

Joy to you, Mariana. Love her, Angelo.

I have confessed her and I know her virtue.

Thanks, good friend Escalus, for thy much goodness.

There's more behind that is more gratulate.

Thanks, provost, for thy care and secrecy.

We shall employ thee in a worthier place.

Forgive him, Angelo, that brought you home

530 The head of Ragozine for Claudio's.

Th'offence pardons itself. Dear Isabel,

I have a motion much imports your good,

Whereto if you'll a willing ear incline,

What's mine is yours, and what is yours is mine.

So, bring us to our palace, where we'll show

What's yet behind, that's meet you all should know.

Exeunt

COMMENTARY

BIBLICAL quotations are from the Bishops' Bible.

In the Commentary and the Account of the Text the abbreviation 'F' is used for the first Folio (1623).

I.1   (stage direction) *Duke*. The Duke's name is given as Vincentio in the 'names of all the Actors' appended to the F text.

6   *lists* bounds

8–9   *But that, to your sufficiency, as your worth is able, | And let them work*. Possibly a line has been omitted. The general sense is: apply yourselves to your duties with a competence matching your authority.

10   *terms* sessions

14   *warp* deviate

17   *with special soul* with absolute conviction

20   *organs* instruments

29   *belongings* capabilities

30   *proper* exclusively

32–3   *Heaven doth with us as we with torches do, | Not light them for themselves*. The oft-repeated claim that this is an echo of Matthew 5.14–16 or Luke 11.33 seems dubious.

36–40   *Nature never . . . thanks and use* Nature never lends her gifts without herself determining the use to which they shall be put

41   *advertise* instruct

46   *first in question* first appointed

48   *metal*. There is a quibble on 'metal' and 'mettle' (which is the F reading) but the amended spelling better fits the imagery of the passage.

51   *with leavened*. The F line (see Collations) is unmetrical and somewhat un-Shakespearian.

    leavened well fermented, carefully considered

54   *prefers* presents

61   *something on* part of

    the way your way

67–72   *I love the people ... affect it*. This, like I.3.7–10, is often taken as a flattering allusion to James I's alleged dislike of crowds, though there seems little positive evidence that he avoided the populace except, quite understandably, when there was an outbreak of plague. *Macbeth*, IV.3.140–59, commonly taken to be a rather less back-handed compliment to James, suggests that there were times when he positively welcomed crowds.

70   *aves* acclamations

78   *the bottom of my place* the basis of my duties

83   *wait upon* accompany

I.2   (stage direction) *Lucio*. In the list of characters added to the F text Lucio is described as 'a fantasticke'. The word may imply a fop, but in Lucio's case it seems more likely to signify someone with an unbridled fantasy or imagination.

2   *composition* agreement

15–16   *the petition ... that prays for peace*. The regular form of grace ended with the petition that God might 'send us peace in Christ'.

27–8   *there went but a pair of shears between us* we were cut from the same cloth

29   *lists* selvages (narrow strips discarded as waste when material is made up)

32   *three-piled* triple napped (the most expensive kind of velvet)

33   *kersey* coarse-woven woollen cloth

    piled. The word puns on baldness and haemorrhoids, both regarded as a legacy of syphilis.

34   *French velvet.* This allusion to the best quality of velvet characteristically glances at 'the French disease' (syphilis) and 'velvet women' (prostitutes).

38–9   *forget to drink after thee.* Lucio will not expose himself to infection by drinking from the same cup.

43   *tainted or free* with or without venereal infection

49   *dolours.* There is a pun on 'dollars'.

51   *French crown.* The pun on baldness and 'the French disease' in line 34 is repeated.

82   *the sweat* sweating sickness (the form of plague most common in the sixteenth and seventeenth centuries)

83   (stage direction) *A Gaoler and Prisoner pass over the stage.* This direction, which is not in F, assumes that Shakespeare intended an action or dumb-show at this point. The *Yonder man* of line 85 is commonly assumed to be Claudio but must surely, on internal evidence, be some other victim of Angelo's *proclamation.* The dragging of prisoners across the stage was fairly common in early drama, and Shakespeare's source, *Promos and Cassandra,* affords two examples.

92   *maid* a young fish (with a pun on *trouts* in line 89)

113   *provost* (the provost-marshal who superintended executions)

121   *The words of heaven.* It is widely accepted that the reference is to Saint Paul's comment on Exodus 33.19, in Romans 9.15–18, but this does little to clarify the meaning. Claudio, who is here bitter and cynical, remarks that authority exacts full retribution from some, while sparing others, yet its actions still pass under the name of justice. The *words of heaven,* thus literally invoked, must surely refer to the Mosaic doctrine of 'An eye for an eye, and a tooth for a tooth', derived, like so much of *Measure for Measure,* from the Sermon on the Mount

126   *scope* liberty

128   *ravin* devour voraciously
       proper bane particular poison

132   *lief* willingly
        foppery foolishness

133   *mortality*. Most editors amend to 'morality', but the F reading, signifying 'deadliness' or 'mortification', is quite acceptable.

143   *looked after* kept close watch upon

146   *She is fast my wife.* Juliet was Claudio's wife by virtue of hand-fasting or pre-contract, though the marriage had not yet been solemnized. Shakespeare himself evidently took advantage of this controversial sixteenth-century practice since he married Anne Hathaway only six months before the birth of their daughter Susanna.

147   *denunciation* public announcement

149   *propagation* augmentation

152   *made them for us* brought them to our point of view

164   *I stagger in* I am uncertain

171–3   *I warrant ... sigh it off.* The F punctuation appears to have misled most editors. Lucio's meaning is: it certainly must be for a name, if the mere sighing of an amorous milkmaid is enough to get you beheaded.

171   *an* if
        tickle precariously

177   *approbation* probation

182   *prone*. Various glosses ('prompt'; 'apt') have been proffered. The general sense of *prone and speechless* seems to be that Isabella's power of persuasion can achieve its object without the need to exert itself.
        dialect language (but here conveying also the sense of 'dialectic', logical persuasion)

189   *tick-tack* (a game in which pegs were driven into holes; here used to signify sexual intercourse)

I.3.3   *complete* so constituted as to be impenetrable

10   *Where youth and cost a witless bravery keeps.* The first Folio is defective: the later ones print 'cost and witless',

which some editors accept. The present reading, which accepts *keeps* as a so-called Northern plural, means: where youth and wealth maintain a foolish ostentation.

12   *stricture* strictness

20   *weeds.* Some editors amend to 'steeds' (though the laws can scarcely apply to horses), and others to 'wills'. Shakespeare, however, was not averse to mixed metaphors, and links 'weeds' with bits or curbs on at least four other occasions.

21   *fourteen.* This is not consistent with Claudio's *nineteen zodiacs* at I.2.167 and may have arisen from misreading of a numeral, either Arabic or Roman.

28   *Dead to infliction* no longer able to be invoked

29–31   *And liberty ... decorum.* The violation of order or degree is a recurring theme with Shakespeare, whose classic exposition of the doctrine is presented in *Troilus and Cressida*, I.3.75–137.

35   *Sith* since

41–3   *Who may ... slander.* Angelo will impose justice in the Duke's name, but Vincentio himself will remain out of sight in order not to discredit that justice.

50   *precise* rigidly puritanical

51   *at a guard with envy* on his guard against malice

53   *Is more to bread than stone.* An echo of Matthew 7.9: 'Or what man is there of you, whom if his son ask bread, will he give him a stone.'

54   *seemers.* Shakespeare often uses 'seem' in the sense of 'pretend' or 'dissemble', and the present usage strongly suggests that Vincentio already suspects Angelo of hypocrisy – an interpretation which receives powerful support from the revelations in III.1.

I.4.5   *the votarists of Saint Clare.* The order of the Poor Clares, founded in 1212 by Saint Francis of Assisi and Saint Clare, imposed a life of poverty, service, and contemplation. It had not, of course, functioned in

England after the Dissolution of the Monasteries in 1536–9, but Shakespeare shows a close knowledge of its regulations.

17   *stead* assist

25   *weary* tedious

30   *make me not your story* do not tell me false tales

32   *lapwing*. The lapwing runs to and fro in order to conceal the location of its nest. Shakespeare, here and in *Much Ado About Nothing*, III.1.24, seems to associate the bird with tittle-tattle and amorous intrigue.

39   *Fewness and truth* to be brief and truthful

42   *seedness* state of being sown

43   *foison* harvest

51–2   *Bore many gentlemen ... action.* Rumours of war are current in the early part of the play (see I.2.1–5,81) but Shakespeare fails to develop them. Their purpose is presumably to establish that Lucio and his friends are aimless semi-military characters not unlike those in *All's Well that Ends Well*.

54   *givings-out* utterances

60   *rebate* make dull

70   *my pith of business* the main purpose of my business

72   *censured* condemned

75–6   *Alas ... good.* Most editors print an interrogation mark after *good*, but the F pointing, which conveys Isabella's conviction of her own helplessness, seems convincing.

82–3   *All their petitions are as freely theirs | As they themselves would owe them* all their petitions are granted as freely as if they themselves had the granting of them

86   *Mother* prioress

II.1.6   *fall* let fall

12   *your*. F reads 'our', which, on the assumption that 'our blood' relates to human nature in general, may be correct.

19   *passing on* passing sentence on

22–3 *what knows . . . thieves?* what does the law itself know of the judgements that have been passed on thieves by other thieves? Line 22 is, however, metrically suspicious, and it may be that the requisite reading is 'what man knows' or 'what judge knows'.

23   *pregnant* obvious, convincing

28   *For* because

34   *Be executed by tomorrow morning.* F's 'by nine to morrow' renders the line hypermetrical and suggests an undeleted alteration. There is no suggestion elsewhere that nine is the hour appointed for Claudio's execution: rather the contrary.

35   *Bring his confessor.* F's 'him' is unmetrical and unnecessary.

36   *pilgrimage* span of life

39   *brakes of office.* F's 'brakes of Ice' is one of the most notorious cruxes in the play and has never been satisfactorily explained. Editors have usually taken lines 38–40 as sententiae, have glossed *brakes* as 'thickets', and have explained *and answer none* as 'have not been called upon to account for their acts'. The present reading assumes that Escalus is referring to the current state of affairs in Vienna, and that the crucial line refers to Vincentio, who has run away from the entanglements or encumbrances of office and maintains an ominous silence.

56   *comes off well* is well spoken

61   *parcel-bawd* part-time bawd

64   *hot-house* bath-house (and, by implication, a brothel)

66   *detest* (that is, protest)

77   *cardinally* (that is, carnally)

85   *misplaces* misuses words

87   *stewed prunes* (a popular dish with prostitutes; the term came to signify prostitutes themselves – hence Pompey's apology)

113   *Come me to* come to

120   *Allhallond Eve* All-hallow Eve (31 October)

122   *a lower chair*. The precise significance of a lower chair has never been satisfactorily defined, and editors usually make sceptical reference to George Steevens's assertion that most houses formerly had a 'low chair' for the use of the sick or the lazy.

123   *Bunch of Grapes* (the name of a room in an inn)

125   *an open room* a public room

140   *this gentleman's face*. Froth's countenance is evidently the subject of the jokes which extend to line 151. It is conceivable that, like Bardolph in the historical plays, he was given a very red face – 'Lucifer's privy-kitchen, where he doth nothing but roast malt-worms'.

148   *supposed* (that is, deposed)

154   *an it like you* if it please you

       respected (that is, suspected)

164   *Justice or Iniquity?* Escalus refers to Elbow, who, like other justices in Elizabethan drama, is notably stupid, and to Pompey, who is likened to Iniquity, sometimes the Vice in Tudor Morality plays. The phrase is somewhat inconsistent since the scene involves an actual Justice who apparently does not participate before line 264.

167   *Hannibal!* Elbow produces his own characteristic misnomer for 'cannibal', but the subsequent jokes linking Pompey with Julius Caesar show that a deliberate allusion to the Carthaginian general is intended here.

195–6   *and you will hang then*. The F reading 'and you will hang them' has baffled commentators, and the present small emendation seems to resolve the difficulties. Escalus, punning on the phrase, 'hang, draw, and quarter', assures Froth that, if he cultivates the acquaintance of tapsters, they will draw him on to evil ways for which he will eventually be hanged.

199   *taphouse* tavern

207   *your bum*. Thickly stuffed trunk-hose were fashion-

able at the time when *Measure for Measure* was
written.

208-9 *Pompey the Great.* Cnaius Pompeius Magnus (106-48
B.C.). He was defeated by Julius Caesar in the Battle of
Pharsalia, and this is alluded to later in the scene
(lines 236-8).

210 *colour it* camouflage it

219 *splay* sterilize

223 *take order* take action

226 *heading* beheading

231 *bay* (the part of a house that lies under a single gable)

237 *shrewd* harsh

264 *Eleven, sir.* The Justice, with his few belated utterances,
is perplexing, and the casual way in which his name is
added to the scene-heading suggests that he may have
been a Shakespearian afterthought. On the other hand,
one of the Justices in *2 Henry IV* is significantly named
Silence, and it is possible that Shakespeare intended
the present Justice to maintain a meaningful silence in
order to establish a symbolic pattern. True justice is
dumb in the corrupt state of Vienna. All that this
Justice communicates is that it is the eleventh hour
(the symbolism is obvious) and that *Lord Angelo is
severe* (over-severe). It would be dangerous to attach
too much significance to the few words which he
speaks, but they remain strangely impressive.

II.2.25 *God save.* The F line as it stands is metrically defective
and the reading ' 'Saue' is suspicious. If, as is likely,
Shakespeare wrote 'God save', the scribe, Ralph
Crane, would have omitted 'God' in accordance with
the Act of Abuses of 1606.

35-6 *I do beseech you, let it be his fault,* | *And not my brother*
I beseech you let my brother's fault, not my brother,
be condemned to death

40 *To fine.* The verb may mean either 'end' or 'diminish'.
Angelo's meaning is that he cannot ignore offences for

which the penalty has already been established by law.

52   *Look what.* Most editors print 'Look, what', which indicates an impatient exclamation, but there is no comma in F and it is possible that Shakespeare intended the idiomatic use of 'look what', meaning 'whatever'.

59   *longs* belongs

65   *slipped* erred

76   *the top of judgement* the Almighty judge

79   *Like man new made* like man at the Creation, before sin had crept into the world. Mercy is seen as part of the breath of life which God breathed into the nostrils of Adam: see Genesis 2.7.

90   *The law hath not been dead, though it hath slept.* The legal maxim '*Dormiunt aliquando leges, moriuntur nunquam*' is attributed to Sir Edward Coke.

95   *a glass* (either a crystal, as commonly used by fortune-tellers, or 'a glass prospective' of the kind used with spectacular effect in Greene's *Friar Bacon and Friar Bungay*)

96   *by remissness new, conceived.* Lines 96–7 are difficult and have been variously emended. The slight change here made in the F pointing (see Collations) distinguishes between evils currently conceived and those which might be conceived as the result of a renewed access of leniency.

112   *pelting* insignificant

120   *glassy essence.* The phrase has been learnedly related to the medieval notion of the human soul as a fragile glass vessel, but the obvious interpretation, man's essence as he himself sees it in a mirror, best fits the context.

123   *laugh mortal* laugh like human beings (if they had spleens like ordinary mortals, that is)

126   *We cannot weigh our brother with ourself* I am not competent to stand in judgement on my brother

132   *Art avised o' that?* have you discovered that? Lucio is

himself a soldier of sorts, and, though Isabella's assurance that *Great men may jest with saints* touches him not, he is perhaps surprised by her knowledge of army procedure.

136   *skins the vice o'th'top* covers the vice on the top with a new skin

149   *sicles* shekels

153   *preservèd souls* the souls of those preserved from evil (that is, Isabella's sister nuns)

159   *Where prayers cross* where prayers are at cross-purposes

165-8 *but it is I . . . virtuous season.* The warm sunshine of the *virtuous season*, or flowering time, causes the violet (Isabella) to flourish, but corrupts the carrion (Angelo) lying beside it.

169   *sense* sensual desire

172   *evils.* Many editors interpret as 'privies', and the *Oxford English Dictionary* suggests that the requisite word may be 'hovels'. The figurative use seems obvious enough without precise definition.

187   *fond* infatuated

II.3.11 *flaws* unruly passions

12   *blistered her report* sullied her reputation

23   *hollowly* falsely

30-34 *lest you do repent . . . stand in fear.* These lines are obscure and possibly corrupt, but the sentence is interrupted anyway. The general sense seems to be that, while true repentance arises from our love of God, false repentance is based on love for ourselves.

33   *spare heaven* spare to offend against heaven

II.4.3 *invention* thought

4   *God.* In view of the line following, it seems likely that the F reading 'heauen' was a substitution occasioned by the Act of Abuses of 1606.

9   *gravity* staidness

12   *for vain* in vain (with a possible pun on 'vane')
        place position of authority

13   *case* outer covering

16–17   *Let's write . . . crest.* The meaning of these lines has
        been much discussed, but no satisfactory interpreta-
        tion has emerged. The present text substitutes a dash
        for the F colon after *crest* on the assumption that
        Angelo's meditation is suddenly interrupted by the
        entry of the Servant.

27   *The general* the populace
        a well-wished king. This is more certainly a compliment
        to James I than are the alleged references at I.1.67–72
        and I.3.7–10.

45   *saucy* lecherous
        coin God's image beget bastard children
        God's image. F reads 'heauens Image', which blurs a
        palpable allusion to Genesis 1.27. Here, as at line 4,
        it is a ready inference that the Act of Abuses led to a
        modification.

48   *in restrainèd means* by forbidden methods

57–8   *Our compelled sins | Stand more for number than accompt*
        the sins which we cannot help committing are reckoned
        by number rather than by weight

73   *And nothing of your answer* and something for which
        you are in no way answerable

79   *these black masks.* Editors have assumed that Angelo
        alludes to the masks worn by women members of the
        audience, but direct reference of this kind is rare in
        Shakespeare. The dramatic effect is enhanced if we
        take the *black masks* to signify Isabella's veil (the Poor
        Clares wear a black veil) and this gives point to
        enshield in line 80.

80   *enshield* shielded, defended (see preceding note)

90   *But in the loss of question* except for the sake of argument

94   *all-binding law.* F's 'all-building-Law' makes reason-
        able sense, but *manacles* in line 93 justifies the emenda-
        tion.

111   *Ignomy* ignominy

112   *two houses* different stock

122   *fedary* confederate

123   *Owe and succeed thy weakness* own and inherit that
       frailty which you attribute to all men

127–8 *Men their creation mar | In profiting by them* men who
       profit by women's frailty debase their own place in
       creation. Woman was thought of as being part of man;
       Genesis 2.21–3.

134   *arrest* take you at

147   *To pluck on others* to test other people

160   *now I give my sensual race the rein* I now give free rein
       to my sensual inclinations. There is probably a pun
       on horse-riding which, in Elizabethan usage, is often
       given a sexual connotation.

162   *prolixious* superfluous

178   *prompture* prompting

III.1.5–41 *Be absolute ... all even.* It has often been urged that
       the Duke's speech voices Shakespeare's own pessimism,
       but that pessimism is not itself verifiable, and the
       interpretation distorts Vincentio's meaning and
       obscures its subtle irony. The Duke bids Claudio re-
       flect on the comforts of death in case it should be his
       lot to die – but, in accordance with the character
       which he assumes throughout the greater part of the
       play, he does not disclose that it is his purpose that
       Claudio shall live.

5   *absolute* resolved

10   *keep'st* dwellest

14   *accommodations* equipment, endowments

17   *worm* snake

24–5   *For thy complexion shifts to strange effects, | After the
       moon* the influence of the moon affects your behaviour
       (thus rendering you *not certain*, that is, mutable, and
       subject to capricious desires)

26   *ingots* bars of gold or silver

29   *bowels* offspring

31   *serpigo* psoriasis, dry tetter

34–6 *for all thy . . . palsied eld.* These obscure lines have
      been variously explained. The general sense seems to
      be that blessed youth turns to unblessed old age, to the
      state of helplessness (Sans teeth, sans eyes, sans taste,
      sans everything) which renders man wholly dependent
      on the charity of others. But the passage may be
      corrupt, and it is a ready inference that F's 'aged' is a
      misprint for 'agued'.

37   *limb* strength of limb

62   *leiger* resident ambassador

63   *appointment* preparations

72   *vastidity* vastness

73   *determined scope* confined limit

78   *entertain.* Of the various possible meanings, 'cherish'
      (*Oxford English Dictionary* entertain, v.11) seems the
      most apt.

92   *appliances* expedients

94   *enew* drive into the water. The verb relates to the way
      in which hawks kill their prey. F reads 'emmew',
      which some editors take to signify 'inmew' (that is,
      coop up).

96   *cast.* The image is usually explained as deriving from
      the casting of urine, so that the word would mean
      'calculate', but the word was also used for the scouring
      of ditches and ponds, though the earliest *Oxford
      English Dictionary* example is 1614. This second mean-
      ing seems to make better sense in the context: if
      Angelo were scoured and made clear he would be seen
      to be a pond as deep as hell.

97   *precise.* The F reading 'prenzie', here and at line 100,
      has baffled most commentators. It is reasonable to
      surmise that the two words looked so much alike in the
      manuscript that the printer took them to be identical.
      In the light of I.3.50, *Lord Angelo is precise* (that is,

puritanical), the present emendation seems reasonable.

100 *guards* trappings. The 'prenzie gardes' of F are here taken to be precious (as befits a deputy ruler), but emendation to 'precise', as in line 97, would be equally tenable on the assumption that Angelo affected the kind of apparel favoured by the Puritans.

111 *affections* passions

113 *force* enforce

118 *perdurably fined* punished eternally

122 *cold obstruction* rigor mortis

124 *delighted* capable of feeling delight

125–31 *To bathe ... horrible.* Claudio's 'dream of death' closely resembles that of Hamlet (III.1.56–88), and its similarities to Dante's Inferno and Milton's Hell have often been remarked upon. But Claudio's meditations are upon Purgatory rather than Hell since he is, by inference, a Catholic, like his sister. The play makes it clear that he is to receive shrift, and there is no reason to suppose that he anticipates total damnation, though his thoughts may turn that way in lines 129–31, which, as they stand in F, are not susceptible of satisfactory explanation.

126 *thrilling* piercing

144 *shield* grant that, ensure that

145 *wilderness* wildness

146 *defiance.* The *Oxford English Dictionary* gloss for this particular passage is 'contempt', but it is equally possible that Isabella disowns Claudio.

164–6 *only he hath made an assay of her virtue to practise his judgement with the disposition of natures* he has made a trial of her virtue only in order to test his ability to judge character

180 *habit* robes

185 *complexion* nature

191 *resolve* inform

195 *discover* expose

198 *avoid* repudiate

167

210   *fearful* afraid

217   *limit of the solemnity* date fixed for the solemnization

224   *combinate* betrothed

228   *pretending* falsely alleging

235   *avail* benefit

246   *refer yourself to this advantage* impose this condition

251   *stead up* sustain

252   *encounter* sexual cohabitation

255   *scaled.* The precise meaning of the word is not clear, and the various glosses include 'weighed', 'stripped of scales' (like a fish), 'thrown into confusion'. The notion of Angelo being weighed in the balance and found wanting is the one that perhaps best accords with the theme and general imagery of the play.

256   *frame* prime

262   *holding up* maintaining

264   *presently* immediately

III.2   Most editors break the Act at this point, thus imposing a distinction which did not exist on the Shakespearian stage. Since there is no reason for supposing that the Duke leaves the stage, even momentarily, adherence to F seems amply justified, but for convenience of reference the conventional scene division is indicated in the margin.

3   *bastard* a sweet Spanish wine (with, of course, an obvious pun)

5   *two usuries.* The *worser* usury is money-lending; the *merriest* is fleshmongering.

8   *fox and lamb skins.* A gown of fox-fur trimmed with lamb-skin was the customary dress for usurers in Shakespeare's day.

9   *stands for the facing* sanctions the trimming

37   *seeming* dissembling

38   *a cord.* Elbow puns on two meanings: (1) the hang-

man's rope; (2) the girdle which is part of the Duke's Franciscan habit.

43   *Pygmalion's images.* Pygmalion, according to classical lore, brought his sculptures to life by falling in love with them. The term is sometimes taken to signify prostitutes, but Lucio's qualifying phrase, *newly made woman,* rather implies virgins ripe for the plucking.

44-5   *extracting it clutched.* This is often taken as referring to the filching of purses, but Lucio is just as likely to mean sexual stimulation.

46   *tune* fashion

47   *trot.* The word usually signifies an old woman, which, in one sense, is what Pompey is. The possibility of a misprint for 'troth' cannot be ruled out.

48   *Is it sad, and few words?* Lucio asks whether melancholy is now the fashion. The play was written at about the time when the character of the 'malcontent' was in vogue.

49   *trick* fashion

51-2   *Procures* pimps

54   *tub.* There is a pun on: (1) the salting of beef; (2) the sweating treatment for the cure of venereal disease.

56   *powdered* pickled

57   *unshunned* inevitable

67   *husband* housekeeper

70   *wear* fashion

72   *mettle.* There is a pun on 'metal' – the iron of the shackles that Pompey will wear in prison.

102   *sea-maid* mermaid

103   *stock-fishes* dried cod. Monstrous births of the kind glanced at by Lucio were a favourite theme in ballads and pamphlets of the period.

105   *motion generative* male puppet (hence sexually impotent)

106   *infallible* unquestionable

109   *cod-piece.* The name given to the flap worn in the front of hose for covering the genitals. The word

sometimes refers, as apparently here, to the genitals themselves.

115 *detected for* charged with

120 *use* custom

  clack-dish. Beggars carried a wooden bowl for the reception of alms. This had a movable lid which they clacked in order to attract notice. Lucio perhaps uses the word in a bawdy figurative sense.

121 *crotchets* peculiarities

124 *inward* intimate

130 *the greater file of the subject* the majority of the people

132 *unweighing* undiscriminating

134 *helmed* directed

135 *upon a warranted need.* The phrase is usually glossed 'if a warrant were necessary', but Shakespeare sometimes used 'upon' in the sense 'in consequence of', and it therefore seems likely that the Duke means that his recent course of action is one for which there was ample warrant.

135–6 *proclamation* reputation

136–7 *bringings-forth* achievements

138–9 *unskilfully* in ignorance

156 *opposite* opponent

162 *For filling a bottle with a tun-dish* for having had sexual intercourse

163–4 *ungenitured* without testicles

169 *untrussing* letting down his hose

171 *eat mutton* cohabit with prostitutes

172 *mouth* kiss erotically

175 *mortality* human life

193 *Philip and Jacob* (1 May: the Feast of Saint Philip and Saint James)

213 *dissolution* total destruction

215–16 *as it is virtuous to be constant in any undertaking.* Vincentio's meaning is presumably that it is now accounted a virtue to be constant in any enterprise, however worthless, though *undertaking* may bear a specifically sexual meaning, as apparently in *Twelfth Night*, I.3.55–6, 'I would not undertake her in this company'.

217–18 *security enough to make fellowships accursed*. Social relationships are cursed by the frequency with which men stand surety for their friends. Vincentio's seemingly casual comment links with the central theme of such plays as *The Merchant of Venice* and *Timon of Athens*.

228 *events* the outcome of his enterprises

232 *sinister* unjust

240 *shore* limit

249–70 These rhyming couplets have often been stigmatized as a non-Shakespearian insertion but their authenticity is nowadays generally accepted. Marston, in *The Malcontent*, I.4.43, has a revealing stage direction, '*Bilioso entering, Malevole shifteth his speech*', and the change of style thus established is also part of Shakespeare's practice. Here Vincentio's shifting of speech is intended to emphasize its preceptive content and also to indicate that the speaker himself is turning from a passive to an active role. He has, at last, begun to grasp the principles of good government.

252 *and* if

253–4 *More nor less to others paying | Than by self-offences weighing* passing judgement on others in accordance with his own imperfections

258 *my vice* the vice that I have allowed to grow up

261–4 *How may likeness ... things!* These lines, sometimes held to be corrupt, are certainly cryptic. F prints them as a question, but they seem more likely to be an apostrophe. I take *likeness* in line 261 to relate back to man's angelic likeness in line 260. *To* in line 263 may be a scribal or compositorial error, and is syntactically difficult. The present text emends F's 'To draw' to *To-draw* on the assumption that Shakespeare intended an archaism (compare Chaucer's 'to-drawen' meaning

171

'to allure' in *Boethius*, Book 4, Metre 3, 46). This admits the rough paraphrase: thus it is that man, outwardly so like an angel, but inwardly criminal, may follow the fashion of the times and, with trivialities, lure to destruction things of weight and value. The lines may refer specifically to Angelo but could just as easily be a generalization.

IV.1.1–6   *Take, O take ... in vain.* These lines, with an additional non-Shakespearian stanza, appear in Fletcher's *The Bloody Brother* (*c.* 1625) with the result that some critics have questioned their authenticity. But it appears to have been Shakespeare's normal practice to write his own songs, and this one is certainly worthy of his genius. A setting of both stanzas by John Wilson (1595–1674) appeared in Playford's *Select musicall ayres* (1652) and is reprinted and usefully discussed in the new Arden edition of *Measure for Measure*, pages 201–3. It cannot, in view of the date of Wilson's birth, have been the version used in early performances of Shakespeare's play.

27   *circummured* walled round

29   *planchèd* planked

30   *his* its

39   *In action all of precept.* This difficult phrase presumably means that Angelo directed Isabella by means of hints, gestures, and perhaps sketch-maps.

41   *observance* compliance

43   *possessed* informed

59–64   *O place and greatness ... in their fancies.* The Duke's seemingly gratuitous meditation is, as Johnson noted, 'a necessity to fill up the time in which the ladies conversed apart'. The sentiments are characteristically Shakespearian and the imagery accords with the concept of '*Rumour*, painted full of tongues' in the induction to *2 Henry IV*.

61   *contrarious quests* conflicting inquiries

64   *rack* put on the rack

71   *He is your husband on a pre-contract.* The contract between Angelo and Mariana, unlike that between Claudio and Juliet, belonged to the category of *sponsalia jurata* and could not be dissolved without the consent of both parties.

74   *flourish* adorn

75   *tilth's.* The F reading 'Tithes' makes some kind of sense but Warburton's emendation is plausible and has won general acceptance.

IV.2.4   *his wife's head.* In Pauline doctrine the husband is the head of the wife (Ephesians 5.23). There is perhaps a pun on maidenheads, as in *Romeo and Juliet*, I.1.21–5.

6   *snatches* quibbles

11   *gyves* fetters

12–13   *unpitied* pitiless

18   *Abhorson.* The name is a curious portmanteau one which combines the words 'abhor' and 'whoreson' and may also pun on 'abortion'.

21   *compound* make terms

26   *mystery* profession

30   *favour* face

40   *Every true man's apparel . . . your thief.* The argument is obscure but turns apparently on the hangman's right to claim the clothes of his victims. The general sense seems to be that the honest man thinks that anything is good enough for the thief while the thief thinks that nothing is good enough for him. But Abhorson's demonstration is manifestly incomplete.

41   *true* honest

55   *yare* prepared

55–6   *a good turn.* A hangman was said to turn off his victims when he removed the ladder from under their feet.

64   *starkly* stiffly

77   *Even with* in exact conformity with
stroke and line. The underlying imagery has been
variously explained, but it seems likely that Shakespeare had no very precise picture in mind. The stroke
and line of justice, though not specifically definable,
seems intelligible enough.

80   *qualify* reduce
mealed stained

84   *steelèd* hardened

86   *th'unsisting postern.* This phrase has produced various
conjectures and emendations, but there seems little
doubt that *unsisting* is an aphetic form of 'unassisting'.
The postern, though a small door, was normally very
strong and certainly 'unassisting'.

89   *countermand* reprieve

95   *siege* seat

107   *quick.* Either Shakespeare was guilty of tautology or the
word must signify 'rash' or 'impetuous'.

114   *putting on* incitement

133   *fact* offence

142   *mortality* death
desperately mortal in a desperate state of mortal sin

153   *cunning* discernment

158   *present* immediate

161   *limited* prescribed

168–9   *discover the favour* recognize the features

171   *tie the beard.* It is not clear that the tying of the beard,
whatever this implies, would have added materially to
the disguise, and many editors have flirted with the
emendation 'dye'. In view of *so bared* in line 172, the
requisite reading may be 'trim'.

183   *fearful* afraid

184   *attempt* tempt

187   *character* handwriting

196   *th'unfolding star* the morning star (the signal for the
shepherd to lead his flock from the fold)

202   *resolve* reassure

IV.3.2 *house of profession* brothel

5 *commodity*. Usurers, in order to obtain more than the lawful interest of ten per cent, devised the system of lending commodities for resale. The various commodities mentioned by Elizabethan writers include lute-strings, hobby-horses, morris-bells, and, as here, ginger and brown paper.

6 *five marks*. The value of the mark was 13s. 4d.

8 *or*. Emendation of F's 'for' seems justifiable since Pompey is musing ironically and not stating a fact.

11 *peaches* impeaches

13 *Copperspur*. Shakespeare evidently recalled, perhaps unconsciously, that a character named Copper appears in *1 Promos and Cassandra*, V.5.

15 *tilter* jouster, fencer

16 *Shoe-tie*. This was apparently a nickname given to travellers, many of whom wore on their shoes the elaborate rosettes fashionable abroad.

18 *'for the Lord's sake'*. This was the customary formula used by prisoners for begging alms from passers-by.

39 *clap into* make haste with

46 *ghostly father* spiritual father, confessor

53 *billets* thick sticks

61 *ward* cell

66 *transport him* send him to his doom

71 *omit* ignore

76 *presently* immediately

77 *Prefixed* stipulated

82 *continue* preserve

87 *journal* daily

yond generation. There have been various attempts to emend or explain this difficult phrase. Perhaps the best explanation is that it refers to the world that lies beyond the darkness of the prison (which never receives the sun's greeting).

89 *free* willing

91 *Varrius*. F prints 'Angelo', but the grounds for emen-

dation are strong: either the scribe or the compositor could have caught up the name from the end of the preceding line; the subsequent scenes make it clear that Angelo and Escalus are to meet Vincentio at the city gates after he has been escorted from the sacred fount, *A league below the city* by Varrius and Friar Peter. Varrius is a minor character, but IV.5.11–13 suggests that he makes some small but vital contribution to the Duke's devices.

98 *By cold gradation and well-balanced form.* The alleged difficulties of this line disappear if we take it as referring to the dénouement devised by the Duke. In the final Act he proceeds against Angelo coldly or impersonally, step by step, and with strict regard to the appropriate formalities.

103 *want* require

117 *close* silent

127 *One of our covent, and his confessor.* Since *Gives* in line 128 may be either singular or plural, it is possible that *One of our covent* and *his confessor* are two different people. This would resolve the problem presented by Friar Thomas in I.3 and the Friar Peter of the latter part of the play. *Already he hath carried* in line 128 may seem to rule this out, but, in the context, *he* could easily refer to the Duke, and *carried* in the sense of 'sent' or 'dispatched' is obviously possible.

 covent convent

128 *instance* indication

131 *pace* direct, train (as a horse)

133 *bosom* wishes

140 *perfect him* relate to him in full

141 *to the head* to the face

143 *combinèd* bound

151 *fain* forced

152–3 *for my head* for fear of being beheaded

153 *set me to't* arouse my sexual desires

155 *fantastical* whimsical

157   *beholding* indebted
160   *woodman* woman-chaser
170   *medlar* prostitute

IV.4.1   *disvouched* contradicted
5   *reliver* hand over. Most editors, following Capell, print 're-deliver', but F's 're-liuer' (from French *relivrer*) is a typical Shakespearian coinage.
11   *devices* false charges
15   *men of sort and suit* men of rank and others normally attendant on the Duke
18   *unpregnant* unready
24   *bears a credent bulk* bears such a weight of conviction
27   *sense* intention

IV.5.1   *deliver me* deliver for me
3   *keep* follow
4   *drift* plan
5   *blench* deviate
8   *Crassus.* Shakespeare evidently picked up the name from Whetstone's *Heptameron* which alludes to 'the two brave Romanes, Marcus Crassus, and Marius'. This also warrants the surmise that *Varrius* may have been a scribal or compositorial error for 'Marius', though such an assumption is far from necessary. The names introduced in this scene well illustrate that Shakespearian 'confusion of the names and manners of different times' which Johnson (wrongly) condemned in *Cymbeline*.

IV.6.4   *to veil full purpose* to conceal the full plan
10   *stand* position
13   *generous* of noble birth
14   *hent* taken their places at

V.1   (stage direction) *at several doors.* The Jacobean stage had doors at either side, and to these there attached a rough but effective symbolism. The Duke, Varrius, and attendant Lords would enter by the one door; the remaining characters by the other.

1   *cousin.* The term, like 'brother' elsewhere in the play, denotes highness of rank, not kinship.

8   *Forerunning more requital* preceding other rewards
     bonds obligations

10   *To lock it in the wards of covert bosom* to imprison it in my innermost heart

13   *razure* erasure

16   *keep* dwell

20   *Vail your regard* lower your eyes

48   *conjure* adjure

50–51   *That thou neglect me not with that opinion | That I am touched with madness* that you do not ignore me because you suppose that I am demented

52   *unlike* unlikely

54   *absolute* perfect

56   *dressings* robes of office
     characts insignia

65   *inequality* injustice

67   *seems* that seems

70   *upon* on account of

82   *perfect* fully prepared

90   *to the matter* pertinent

94   *refelled* refuted

98   *concup'scible* sensual
     intemperate ungoverned

100   *remorse* compassion

105   *fond* foolish

107   *practice* conspiracy

108   *it imports no reason* it does not make sense

110   *proper* applicable

118   *countenance.* The word is variously explained as 'privilege', 'pretence', but the requisite meaning may be

'acceptance' (compare the common Elizabethan verb 'to countenance').

126   *A ghostly father, belike.* Since the title *Friar Lodowick* signifies that he is a ghostly, or spiritual, father, the Duke must intend an ironical pun. Hence *ghostly* here means 'non-existent'.

130   *swinged* whipped (from 'to swinge')

131   *This'* this is

145   *a temporary meddler* a meddler in temporal (as opposed to spiritual) affairs

157   *probation* proof

158   *convented* summoned

160   *vulgarly* publicly

179   *punk* harlot

186   *known* had sexual knowledge of

209   *match* appointment

217   *proportions* dowry

218   *composition* the agreed sum

219–20   *disvalued | In levity* discredited for wantonness

231   *I did but smile till now.* Angelo's smile has already been mentioned at II.2.186–7: *Ever till now, | When men were fond, I smiled and wondered how.* Both passages have sinister reverberations and suggest that the image of 'the smiler with a knife' was, for Shakespeare, a deeply personal one. Examples occur elsewhere in the plays, notably in *Hamlet*, I.5.108: 'That one may smile, and smile, and be a villain'.

234   *informal* demented

240   *Compact* confederate

243   *approbation* proof

254   *your injuries* the matters alleged against you

256   *leave, but.* F prints 'leaue you; but' which is otiose and results in mislineation.

257   *Determinèd* reached a judgement

261   *Cucullus non facit monachum* the hood does not make the monk. This proverb, signifying that appearances

are sometimes deceptive, was common in various forms in Shakespeare's day.

265   *enforce* urge

266   *notable fellow*. Both words were often used in a pejorative sense, and here signify a 'notorious rascal'.

274   *handled her privately*. Lucio's tasteless sexual puns contrast oddly with his view of Isabella as *a thing enskied and sainted* at I.4.34, but he is, of course, the complete opportunist.

277   *darkly* cunningly

278   *light* wanton

290–91   *Respect to your great place, and let the devil | Be sometime honoured for his burning throne*. These lines have been much disputed and the F text may be corrupt. But 'and' in Shakespearian English sometimes stands for 'and also' or 'and even', and either of these senses would be appropriate here. The Duke is openly defiant, and what he is, in effect, saying is: I am willing to honour your authority and even that of the devil himself.

291   *burning throne*. The lines in *Antony and Cleopatra*, II.2.195–6, 'The barge she sat in, like a burnish'd throne, | Burn'd on the water', suggest that Shakespeare was as much concerned with the actual splendour of the devil's seat as with the more usual implications of hell-fire.

299   *retort* throw back

306   *proper* very

307   *glance* turn

309   *touse* tear

311   *hot* hasty

314   *provincial* subject to local jurisdiction

317   *stew*. The word, part of Vincentio's hell-broth imagery, also puns on 'stew' meaning brothel.

319–20   *Stand like the forfeits in a barber's shop, | As much in mock as mark*. Shakespeare evidently recalled the somewhat pointless barber's shop scene in *1 Promos and Cassandra*, V.5. The *forfeits* have been explained either as teeth, extracted by barbers and threaded on lute-strings, or as a semi-comic list of penalties that a customer was liable to incur. Since the word itself is vague, and since barbers acted also as dentists and surgeons, neither explanation is compelling. The Barber-Surgeons' Company was entitled to receive the corpses of executed criminals for dissection purposes, and this suggests that the *forfeits*, which were supposed to stand as *mark* ('warning'), were of distinctly gruesome character.

330   *notedly* particularly

332   *coward*. No such charge has hitherto been alleged against the Duke.

339   *close* compromise

343   *bolts* fetters

344   *giglots* harlots

351   *sheep-biting face*. Lucio likens the Duke to the proverbial wolf in sheep's clothing, who employs the disguise in order to prey upon the flock.
       hanged. Hanging, the customary punishment for sheep-stealing, was extended to dogs and, in folk-lore, to other predatory animals.

360   *or . . . or . . . or* either . . . or . . . or

367   *passes*. The various editorial glosses, for example, 'course of action', 'devices', 'events' are all plausible, but the tone of the whole passage suggests that Shakespeare intended the word to signify 'trespasses'.

380   *Advertising* attentive
       holy devoted

382   *Attorneyed* bound (as by law)

389   *remonstrance* revelation

393   *brained* killed

398   *salt* lecherous

404   *The very mercy of the law* the law, even when interpreted with extreme mercy

405   *proper* very

410   *denies.* I take this to be a so-called Northern plural in apposition to *faults* (line 409).

424   *definitive* immovable

430   *sense* natural feeling

431   *fact* crime

432   *pavèd bed.* The implication is, presumably, that Claudio has been buried under the pavement of the prison.

450   *subjects.* The word has been variously explained, but the context strongly suggests that it simply means 'deeds': compare line 448.

461   *advice* reflection

468   *still* hitherto

479   *And squar'st thy life according* and pattern out your life accordingly

480   *quit* remit

483   *muffled.* Claudio, as *another prisoner*, is likely to have been brought on blindfold, but it is possible that a more ample disguise is implied since it is important that Isabella should not recognize her brother until he is unmuffled at line 486.

490   *But fitter time for that.* Dr Johnson and subsequent editors have been perturbed 'that Isabel is not made to express either gratitude, wonder or joy at the sight of her brother', but the Duke's insistence on a *fitter time* may explain why this is so. Shakespeare's comic dénouement is sometimes made to sacrifice sentiment in the interests of technical dexterity. There is a sufficiently close parallel in *Cymbeline*, V.5.104–5, where Imogen dismisses her benefactor, Lucius, with the words 'your life, good master, | Must shuffle for itself'.

493   *quits* requites

494   *her worth worth yours* making your worth equal to hers

495   *an apt remission* a readiness to pardon

498   *luxury* lechery

502   *trick* current fashion
526   *more behind* more to come
         gratulate gratifying
532   *motion* project

AN ACCOUNT OF THE TEXT

Measure for Measure was first printed in the Shakespeare Folio of 1623 and there is good reason for believing that the copy which reached the printing-house was a transcript of an autograph manuscript prepared by Ralph Crane, a professional scrivener who is known to have done a fair amount of work for Shakespeare's company. The current view is that, in 1621, when work on the Folio began, four compositors of varying reliability set up the text of *Measure for Measure* from a transcript exemplary in its neatness and legibility but subject to the peculiarities and occasional inaccuracies that adhere to Crane's extant manuscripts.

In fairness to Crane it must be conceded that his task may not have been an easy one. There is ample evidence to show that his transcript was not based on the theatre prompt-book, and it is likely that he was forced to work from an untidy, and possibly unperfected, Shakespearian draft which had suffered a measure of deterioration.

All in all, there is good sense in Dr Johnson's comprehensive judgement that 'there is perhaps not one of Shakespeare's plays more darkened than this by the peculiarities of its author, and the unskilfulness of its editors, by distortions of phrase, or negligence of transcription'. The Folio text provides a number of the most notorious Shakespeare cruxes and throughout there are readings which, though not demonstrably wrong, arouse suspicion. It has been customary for editors to allow certain unintelligible readings to stand for the sufficient reason that no tolerable alternatives have so far suggested themselves. Such conservatism is, on the whole, reflected in the text of the present edition but, in view of current opinions about transmission, various minor emendations have been made, mainly on the principle that metrically defective lines may readily be attributed to Crane or the compositors, but, under no circumstances, to Shakespeare.

COLLATIONS

I

The selective list of collations which follows attempts to indicate all significant deviations from the F text. Readings which appear to be peculiar to the present edition are marked '*this edition*'. The F reading is given on the right of the square bracket.

I.1.	48	metal] mettle
	50	upon't (*this edition*)] vpon it
	51	with leavened (*this edition*)] with a leauen'd
I.2.	45–6	I have . . . come to –] *given to Lucio in* F
	114	*marked as* '*Scena Tertia*' *in* F
	147	do denunciation (*this edition*)] doe the denunciation
	171	is, an (*this edition*)] is: And
I.3.	10	cost a witless] cost, witlesse
	26–7	rod | Becomes more] rod | More
	42	sight] fight
	43	it] in
	46	instruct] instruct me
	47	bear me] beare
I.4.	5	sisterhood] Sisterstood
	30	It is] 'Tis
	54	givings-out] giuing-out
	74	for his] For's
	78	make] makes
II.1.	12	your] our
	34	by tomorrow (*this edition*)] by nine to morrow
	35	Bring his (*this edition*)] Bring him his

II.1.   39   brakes of office (*this edition*)] brakes of Ice
       196   then (*this edition*)] them
       249   your] the
II.2.   3   he'll (*this edition*)] he will
         6   for it] for't
  25, 161   God save] 'Saue
        58   call it back again] call it againe
        80   condemns] condemne
        92   If that the] If the
        96   remissness new, conceived (*this edition*)] remis-
             senesse, new conceiu'd
        99   ere] here
       107   'tis (*this edition*)] it is
       111   ne'er] neuer
II.4.   4   God] heauen
         9   seared] feared
        17   crest – (*this edition*)] Crest:
        24   swoons] swounds
        45   God's (*this edition*)] heauens
        48   metal] mettle
        53   or] and
        58   than accompt] then for accompt
        75   craftily] crafty
        76   Let me be] Let be
        94   all-binding law] all-building-Law
       103   long I have] longing haue
   112–13   mercy is | Nothing] mercie, | Is nothing
       153   world] world aloud
III.1.   55   me to hear them] them to heare me
        72   Though] Through
        94   enew] emmew.
        97   precise] prenzie
        99   damnèd'st] damnest
       100   precious (*this edition*)] prenzie
       133   penury] periury
       216   to her by oath] to her oath
III.2.   23   eat, array] eate away

III.2.   37   Free from our] From our
          38   waist] wast
        44–5   extracting it clutched] extracting clutch'd
         143   dearer] deare
       171–2   He's not past it yet] He's now past it, yet
         209   See] Sea
         215   as it is] and as it is
IV.1.   53   and so have] and haue
          61   quests] Quest
          75   tilth's] Tithes
IV.2.   40–44 If it be . . . your thief] *given to Pompey in* F
          55   yare] y'are
          98   lordship's] Lords
         140   reckless] wreaklesse
IV.3.   8   or (*this edition*)] for
          15   Forthright] *Forthlight*
          16   Shoe-tie] *Shootie*
          91   Varrius (*this edition*)] *Angelo*
          98   well-balanced] Weale-ballanc'd
IV.4.   24   bears a] beares of a
IV.5.   8   Valentius] *Valencius*
V.1.   13   me] we
          95   vile] vild
         168   her face] your face
         256   leave, but (*this edition*)] leaue you; but
       256–7   have well | Determinèd] have | Well determin'd
         409   faults] fault's
         420   confiscation] confutation

2

The following stage directions (or parts of directions) do not
appear in F. Minor additions such as '*aside*', '*to Juliet*', '*sings*'
are not listed here.

I.2.   83   *A Gaoler and Prisoner pass over the stage*
II.1.   36   *Exit Provost*

MORE ABOUT PENGUINS, PELICANS,
PEREGRINES AND PUFFINS

For further information about books available from Penguins please write to
Dept EP, Penguin Books Ltd, Harmondsworth, Middlesex UB7 ODA.

In the U.S.A.: For a complete list of books available from Penguins in the
United States write to Dept DG, Penguin Books, 299 Murray Hill Parkway,
East Rutherford, New Jersey 07073.

In Canada: For a complete list of books available from Penguins in
Canada write to Penguin Books Canada Ltd, 2801 John Street, Markham,
Ontario L3R 1B4.

In Australia: For a complete list of books available from Penguins in Australia
write to the Marketing Department, Penguin Books Australia Ltd, P.O. Box
257, Ringwood, Victoria 3134.

In New Zealand: For a complete list of books available from Penguins in New
Zealand write to the Marketing Department, Penguin Books (N.Z.) Ltd,
Private Bag, Takapuna, Auckland 9.

In India: For a complete list of books available from Penguins in India write to
Penguin Overseas Ltd, 706 Eros Apartments, 56 Nehru Place, New Delhi
110019.

NEW PENGUIN SHAKESPEARE

General Editor: T. J. B. Spencer